MURDER IN MAGIC CITY

A CONNOR COLE MYSTERY

BRYAN PEABODY

SALTY SEA PRESSS

To Clara, for always believing in me.

FOREWORD

Today, Miami is a massive metropolitan tourist destination. A place that most people think of for sun,
sand, the glitz and glamor of South Beach, and the
rich and famous lifestyle.

But over one-hundred years ago it was not much
more than a swamp. The Miami area grew from just
over one thousand residents to nearly five and a half
million in just one-hundred and ten years.

The city's nickname, "The Magic City", comes from
this rapid growth. Winter visitors, when seeing the
population change from year to year on their arrival,
remarked that the city grew so much and so quickly,
that it was like magic.

The nickname has stuck ever since.

1

I woke up to the bright Miami sun warming my face. This was the result of a long night of staring into a laptop screen, a little too much rum, and me forgetting to close the blinds when I finally couldn't keep my eyes open any longer. Not a bad way to wake up really but I would have preferred a few more hours of sleep.

I slowly opened one eye and had to squint due to the bright sun. When the clock finally came into focus, I saw it read 8:07am. Normally the only time I like seeing the hour start with an "8" is if it's followed by "pm".

But this morning I don't mind quite as much. Last night I finished an investigation I was consulting on for the FBI and it's time to show the suits what I found. And of course, my favorite part of any consultation, collecting the paycheck. Which I could really use soon.

"Hey papi, close the blinds, por favor."

That's Sophia, she helps on cases now and again. In my line of work, I've found that people tend to say things to pretty women that they won't say to me, which is obviously something handy to have around. She's also never met a lock she couldn't pick and she's almost as good of an investigator as me. Two things I look for in a partner.

She also stays over from time to time. I wouldn't exactly say we are dating but I wouldn't exactly say we aren't either. I've never really figured out what we are, but some things you just don't question. Mostly because you might not like the answer you get.

Now, I know what you're probably thinking. Mixing business with pleasure is never a great idea, and you're probably right. But I've never been one to make the best choices, especially when it comes to women.

I slowly swung my legs around and sat on the side of the bed rubbing my eyes, trying to convince my legs to wake up and start moving. When they finally did, my bare feet felt the cool tile floor and I thought for a second about getting back into bed with Sophia. But I know Sophia will give me shit if I don't make my meeting today. Mostly, I suspect, because she needs the paycheck almost as much as me.

As my legs finally got some feeling of life in them, I stood up, stretched, and walked over to close the blinds.

"Gracias papi", Sophia mumbled, still half asleep. I managed to grumble a "uh huh", in response, as I headed for the kitchen to look for breakfast.

An empty refrigerator greeted me as I opened the door, except for a half full bottle of Coke and a half-eaten bag of bite-sized snickers. I guess that will have to do.

"I have to get some groceries when I get paid today", I said out loud to myself.

Five bite-sized snickers and a juice glass of Coke later, Sophia stumbled out of the bedroom wearing one of my white t-shirts and black boy shorts. She looked at me, then at the empty snicker wrappers lying on the counter.

"Really? That's your breakfast?" she said, raising one eyebrow, showing her disapproval.

"Yeah, there isn't anything else in the fridge. And besides, a Snickers really satisfies", I said with a laugh.

I thought this was amazingly funny at this hour of the morning, but I don't think Sophia was amused; she gave me a smirk and an eye roll as she turned and left the room.

"Papi", Sophia yelled from the bedroom, "what's the plan for today? You finished the work on that FBI case last night, right?"

"Yeah, it's done. I'm leaving in a bit to meet with Special Agent Matthew Banks", I said.

"He also told me that he has a lead for me on another case. It isn't for the FBI, some friend of his, I think. He said he'd fill me in later today. I'm a little surprised that guy has any friends at all."

"You know", Sophia interrupted, "you have multiple university degrees and you ran your own company. You could be working at some big firm or running your own company again, instead of living paycheck to paycheck chasing criminals."

Sophia hit a nerve, after what happened with the company I owned, but I wasn't going to show her I was annoyed.

"I could be, but I prefer dealing with criminals to sitting in an office and dealing with type-A assholes all day. You know how they are. Besides, I wouldn't have met you if I were working at one of those places."

"And, who would make sure that I eat a healthy breakfast if you weren't around?" I teased, trying my best not to be annoyed.

As I talked, I packed my laptop into my backpack, double checked that the thumb drive for Agent Banks was in my pocket and then grabbed my helmet when I saw Sophia poke her head around the corner.

"And speaking of a healthy breakfast, when the FBI pays you today, be sure to go buy some real food with the money. Snickers and Coke don't count."

"Claro, claro" I said as I headed for the door.

The early summer heat in Miami was already brutal and the humidity hit me in the face like a ton of bricks as soon as I stepped outside. Every once in a while, I have to remind myself that living in paradise and dealing with the summer heat is much preferable to ice and snow.

As I pulled on my helmet and started the motorcycle, I couldn't help but think that Sophia had a point. My former life had afforded me things, like paying cash for the motorcycle I was riding and the condo I live in. Not to mention lavish parties and mingling with the rich and famous.

But that life is over now. And, as much as I miss a steady, well-paying paycheck, I can't go back to that life again. Especially after how it ended.

I shook my head a couple of times to clear the thoughts of the past and pulled out of the driveway.

FBI headquarters was a twenty-minute drive from my place in Hialeah Gardens. This time of day most of the work traffic has died down and it's a mostly smooth ride up I-75 North.

I slowed the bike down, exited off the interstate and made a left onto 145th Avenue.

You can't miss the FBI headquarters building. Every time I see it, it reminds me of a cubist painting. Everything looks funny and at odd angles but some-how, it just works.

I slide the visor on my helmet up as I came to a stop at the security check point. A large security guard lumbered out of the guard shack and looked at me.

"Can I help you, sir?" he said, eyeing me a bit oddly. I assume they probably don't get a lot of people on motorcycles here.

"My name is Connor Cole. I have an appointment with Special Agent Matthew Banks this morning."

The guard stepped back inside and called the main building to confirm my appointment. A minute later he returned.

"Yes sir, he's expecting you. Drive up to guest parking and go to the reception desk in the main lobby."

I nodded and as the gate raised, I spotted guest parking.

2

I opened the door leading into the main lobby and the cool air conditioning was a welcome relief from the heat. As I walked through the door, Maria, the receptionist for the building, and I caught each other's eye. She flashed a smiled as I walked towards her.

Maria was in her late twenties, tall and thin, with dark eyes and hair. I always imagined that she moon-lighted as a Victoria Secret model with those looks. She has always been my favorite part of coming to meet with the FBI. Well, second favorite, after the paycheck.

"Hello, Mr. Cole. It's been a while, how have you been?" she asked.

"Nice to you see you again Maria, it has been a while. What's it been, maybe a couple months now? Did you miss me?" I teased playfully.

"Maybe a little", she said with a smile, "I think the last time was at my cousins wedding that you accompanied me to. That was a fun night", she said with a wink.

"You're here to meet with Agent Banks, aren't you?"

"I am. I have some research to drop off for a case he is working on."

Maria got up from her seat, walked around the desk and lightly slid her hand down my arm as she walked by and said "I'll let him know you're here, guapo. I'll be right back."

When she reached the door, she looked back over her shoulder and saw me watching her walk away. She gave me a satisfied smile and disappeared through the door.

Maria has a way about her that makes it difficult for me to keep my mind on anything other than her. Really, when it comes to women in general, I'm easily distracted by most of them.

"Focus Cole. Focus. You're here for a job", I had to remind myself. And not for the first time either, if you want the truth.

A few minutes later Special Agent Matthew Banks walked into the lobby. He fit the exact description of how I'd describe an FBI agent: Tall and well-built. I'd guess around forty years old with short, tight cut hair, a cheap suit and could be a bit of a hard ass. I could easily imagine him in the military. For all I knew, he was ex-military. Everything about him screamed fed.

He has worked cyber-crimes for several years now and usually ends up with cases that involve some sort of technology that he doesn't understand. Which was hardly surprising; I wouldn't be surprised if he had a hard time working his microwave. But I'm not complaining, I've made good money working as a consultant for him. Not to mention helping him clear a high percentage of his cases because of me. Something I enjoy reminding him of from time to time, especially when he's being a smart ass. Which is most of the time.

"Mr. Cole. I hope you have good news for me", he said with a scowl, getting straight to the point.

I reached out and shook his hand, "And it's good to see you too, Agent Banks", I said dryly, "I think you'll be happy with what I have for you. The information is on a thumb drive and my laptop is in my bag. I can walk you through it; it shouldn't take but a couple of minutes."

I took out my laptop and inserted the thumb drive to show Agent Banks what I had found the night before.

"Your suspicions about someone compromising the firms' network security was right. It took a while but combing through access and database logs, I was able to track the hacker. He hid his tracks well, but I eventually tracked him to an IP address in Chicago. The local ISP should be able to pinpoint where the user lives with it, no problems. Your guys in the Chicago office shouldn't have any trouble after that", I explained.

"From what I could tell, the firms' research database was the target. I assume it's something valuable to go to this much trouble, do you have any idea what they were looking for?" I asked.

"I do but that, I'm afraid, is above your pay grade. Well done Mr. Cole. I'd say you earned your consulting fee with this; it looks like it was a lot of time spent digging", Agent Banks said.

"Yeah, that it was", I agreed.

"OK Cole, your check is at the front desk with Maria. You can pick it up on your way out. Oh, and your bag of Snickers is being sent to your home address. Why do you always insist on a bag of Snickers as part of your consulting fee? You do realize you aren't a nine-year-old, right?"

I laughed, "Everyone has a quirk or two Agent Banks and that's mine. Before I forget, you also mentioned that you have a friend that might have some work for me?"

"Ah, yes, I did. The guy's name is Simon Dubois. He's not exactly a friend, more of an acquaintance of mine and the CEO of a Belgium company called NouveauFusion. The company has an office in Miami and Simon lives here most of the year now."

I interrupted, "How does a Belgium company and CEO end up here?"

"The same reason as most people I imagine. They are attracted to the weather, the sun and sand or maybe just the lifestyle", Agent Banks said.

"Simon opened the Miami office about a year ago. The company has office space downtown in the Southeast Financial Center building on South Biscayne Boulevard. Here is his card, I told him to expect your call later today."

"Do you know what they do?" I asked as I took the business card.

"I only know a little. Their main business is around making microchips and software that uses them. My understanding is that they have some new type of microchip that is supposed to be the next big thing. The official description is that the chip contains personal identification information and works like RFID."

"Basically", Banks continued, "it broadcasts your information to anyone or any device that is listening nearby. A typical use, I'm told, is that it can be used like an old-school ID badge, granting or denying access to areas of a building. But instead of a typical card you wear on your person and swipe in front of a card reader to get access to a secure area, the chip is implanted in your hand and contains much more data about you."

I interrupted, "That sounds like a personal privacy nightmare to me. Governments and law enforcement could use that to track people. I could also see hacker groups being particularly interested in the technology too. Are people really willing to have minor surgery to have this thing implanted as a job requirement?"

"I can't really answer that other than Simon said it's the next big thing. So, maybe it's not a big deal. I don't know Cole", Agent Banks answered flatly.

"Did he say what he wants me to do for him?" I asked.

"About a week ago the company had a break-in. The intruder knocked out the security cameras on the floor and bypassed the door security. Simon thinks the company network was accessed and sensitive information was taken. The building security guard discovered the break-in and was shot with a taser by the intruder. The security guard is fine but unfortunately he didn't get a good look at his assailant, other than reporting he thinks he saw a black hoodie."

"That isn't much to go on", I said.

"You're right and to make it worse, Miami PD investigated but came up with nothing. Because Nouveau-Fusion couldn't show anything was stolen, they said there wasn't anything they could do", Agent Banks explained.

"Simon will give you more details but he is interested in having you investigate the possible theft and, if you find evidence of a theft, following the lead to wherever it goes. I told him you were the best guy for the job. Don't let that go to your head, Cole."

I laughed, "I'll do my best."

"See that you do", Agent Banks said looking serious now.

"Give Simon a call this afternoon. I know he's anxious to have you start."

Agent Banks escorted me to the main lobby, thanked me again for my work and reminded me to pick up my check from Maria.

"Well, Mr. Cole, I believe there is something you want from me, right?" Maria said with a playful smirk.

I laughed, "Yes, guapa, I believe there is".

Maria opened a drawer in her desk, took out a paper check and handed it to me. As I reached out to grab it, she pulled it back.

"I need something from you too, Mr. Cole. Call me this weekend and we can discuss it?" she said with a smile.

"Absolutely", I said, as she finally handed me the check.

The bright midday sun nearly blinded me as I left the building and I had to squint as I crossed the parking lot to my bike. I reached into my pocket and took out the card Agent Banks gave me. The card was a classy, all black business card with a shiny finish. It read:

"Simon Dubois, CEO, NouveauFusion"

With an office and cell number, along with the company's Miami address, at the bottom.

I took my phone out of my pocket and dialed the cell number.

After a few rings, Simon answered.

"Hello, Simon Dubois here", he said, with a slight French accent.

"Mr. Dubois, my name is Connor Cole. I was given your number by Special Agent Matthew Banks. He mentioned you were interested in talking to me about the recent break-in at your company."

"Yes, Mr. Cole, thank you for calling. I assume Matthew filled you in on the details?" Simon asked.

"Yes, he did, but I'd like to go over them with you in more detail when you have some free time. As well as see where the break-in occurred."

"That would be fine", Simon said, "I have some meetings this afternoon and a dinner meeting at 6pm. How does 9pm at my office sound to you?"

"That would be fine", I said.

"Excellent, see you then Mr. Cole."

3

It was still several hours before my meeting downtown so I decided to head home and see what I could find out about Simon and NouveauFusion. When I arrived, Sophia was sitting in the kitchen, working on her laptop. She smiled when I came in.

"How did it go papi?", she said.

"Good, I met with Agent Banks and explained what I had found. He seemed happy with it. I picked up the consulting check too. Oh, that reminds me, did anything get delivered today?"

"Yeah, there is a box for you over there", Sophia said, pointing to the couch. "What is it?"

As I picked up the box, I took a knife from my pocket and slid the blade down the top of the box.

"This is the second part of my consulting fee", I said, as I pulled out the giant bag of bite-sized snickers and held it up for Sophia to see.

Sophia rolled her eyes.

"Connor, why do you insist that Banks send you a bag of Snickers every damn time? You are an adult, you know."

"Yeah, I know, but it pisses Banks off and I really enjoy that part", I said with a laugh.

"I have no doubt that you do. What about the other case you mentioned?" she asked.

"Banks knows a guy downtown, Simon.... something. Anyway, his company had a break-in recently. He thinks that some sensitive information was stolen from the company computers. I have a meeting with him later tonight", I replied.

"What's the name of the company", Sophia asked.

"NouveauFusion, have you heard of it?", I asked curiously.

"No, I haven't but maybe you should give Marko a call. If something of value got stolen, he is usually one of the first to know about it. Maybe he can give you an idea about what's going on over there", Sophia said.

"Yeah, assuming he picks up. The last time I talked to him he told me that our cases always end up being more trouble than they are worth to him", I said, "Plus, he isn't the biggest fan of the cops."

I took my phone out of my pocket, scrolled through the contact list and clicked on Marko's number. After two rings, he answered.

"Well, well, Connor Cole, it's been a while. What's happening, tio? I bet you need some help again", Marko said in an annoyed voice. "Why is it that I only hear from you when you need something?"

I laughed, "Good to hear your voice too, Marko. Mostly I could just use some information. Sophia reminded me that you always have an ear to the ground on, shall we say, the shadier happenings around town. So, who better to get information from?"

"Flattery will get you everywhere amigo", Marko said with a laugh and continued, "What kind of information are you looking for?"

"A guy named Simon Dubois; he owns a company called NouveauFusion, I'm told he does something with RFID. He's been in town for about a year now and --"

Marko interrupted, "Mierda, Connor! Why is it that you always want help with the worst possible stuff?"

"You know me, Marko, I lead an interesting life," I said with a slight chuckle to ease the tension before continuing. "Tell ya what, why don't we meet up for a drink this afternoon? I'm buying."

"Damn right you're buying. And you know I only drink the high-end stuff so make sure you bring your wallet. There is a bar in Little Havana called The Ball & Chain. Let's say we meet there in an hour?"

"Perfect. See you then." I agreed.

The Ball & Chain is in the heart of Little Havana on Calle Ocho, right across from Domino Park. On the weekends the place is crazy with an overflowing crowd and live music. This afternoon, in the middle of the work week, there wasn't much happening.

I parked my bike right in front and walked to the door. As I grabbed the door handle, I noticed a flyer advertising live Salsa music this weekend. I'll have to remember to mention that to Sophia, she loves live Salsa music. She will probably try to get me to dance though, like always. "There isn't much I hate more than dancing", I thought to myself.

As I walked in, my eyes needed a few seconds to adjust to the darkened interior. When they did, I saw Marko waving at me from the bar to come over.

"Hola Marko, how's it going?", I said.

"Todo bien, you?", he asked.

"Can't complain man", I answered.

Marko continued, "I just ordered a shot of Patrón, let me get you one too, since you're buying."

"How's that hot little Latina you have helping you out, Sophia is her name, right? When she gets tired of you and is ready for a real man, I'm available", Marko said with a laugh.

"Yeah, Sophia, that's right. She's great. But she isn't interested in a loser like you", I said jokingly and gave him a friendly slap on the back.

Marko laughed and said, "Damn good to see you again, Connor."

"You too brother, you too."

Marko motioned to the bartender and asked her to bring me the same thing he was drinking. Then he turned to me.

"Listen man, about Simon and NouveauFusion, you might want to watch your back on this one." His expression now changed from lighthearted to serious.

"Simon and his company do make RFID technologies, like you were told. What you don't know is that

Simon is a brilliant scientist and has a lot of interest in transhumanism. In fact, it's more than just interest, he's one of the leading researchers in the community. I've heard rumors that his company and making RFID technology, is just a way to fund his other research."

"What the hell is transhumanism?" I asked dumbfounded.

"It's a vision of the future. A group of people that believe that humans can, and should, embrace technology to improve their lives. The next evolution of humanity", Marko started to explain.

I interrupted, "Aren't we already doing that with smart phones, the internet and the rest?"

"That's not what I'm talking about. This is something different. It's much more than using personal technology to make daily life easier."

Marko picked up his shot glass and downed his Patrón, then continued.

"There are several different groups that are pursuing different agendas. For example, one of the more popular ideas is life extension through genetic engineering. Some of these groups believe that long life, or possibly eternal life, is a real possibility."

"Others are interested in tech that can boost our physical or intellectual capabilities beyond what we would consider naturally human."

I laughed, "It sounds like you are describing something straight out of science fiction. You know, the stuff that is just make-believe."

"It sounds just like it but don't be so quick to dismiss it. Did you know that there have already been examples of some of this working?", Marko paused for a second to let that sink in.

"The military experimented with sending a very weak electric current through the brains of their people; it's called trans-cranial direct-current stimulation. It's a mouthful, but the idea is that the current would speed up reaction and learning times. And it worked. The US Air Force put that research to work with their drone pilots and it halved their learning and reaction time. DARPA has used it to speed up the training of snipers. In less violent examples, there are also studies that show it can have useful therapeutic effects on people with neurological issues like Parkinson's disease or stroke victims with motor problems."

"Are you serious?" I asked skeptically, raising an eyebrow in disbelief.

"I am. A lot of this stuff is more real than most people realize. There are several more areas of interest; and some are crazier sounding than others. On the extreme end is one group that believes soon you will be able to upload your memories, experiences, everything, to a computer and essentially live forever.

"And there are your Battlestar Galactica Cylons. I knew it", I said with a laugh.

"Yeah, and it's weird as hell. Hell, all of this is weird, it's just varying degrees", Marko added.

I thought for a moment before continuing as the bartender placed a shot glass in front me.

"All of this would seem to come with major ethics questions. I mean, if people lived an extraordinarily long life, do people stop having kids so the planet doesn't become overcrowded? If not, what will happen? And if we could increase our intelligence to super-human levels, what happens to the people that can't afford it?", I asked.

"You're right, and there is even a branch of transhumanists that are interested in and studying those exact issues", Marko added.

"I guess when you think about it, after the initial weirdness wears off, most of this really isn't as far-fetched as it first seems. Technology moves at a staggering pace. Add to that advances in biomedicine and I guess I could see these becoming real issues that we could have to face in the next decade or two", I said.

"I agree. Think back to when a horse and buggy were considered cutting edge and the best way to get around. When the first car was built, people saw it and thought it was weird too, that it wouldn't last. When was the last time you saw a horse and buggy going down the road? Everything becomes normal with enough time", Marko said.

"The only difference is the car didn't change what it means to be fundamentally human", I added.

"True", Mark paused for a few seconds, then continued.

"One other thing I should add, and this might be of interest to you. I've heard that there is some infighting between the younger generation of transhumanists and the older generation. They have different ideas as to what it all means and what they see as the future. I haven't heard of anything violent, but you never know. So, just a heads up."

"So, maybe someone didn't like what Simon was working on and took it on themselves to stop it", I said.

Marko shrugged, "It's possible."

I glanced at my phone, 8:05pm showed on the display. Only a little less than an hour until I'm due to meet Simon at his office.

"I need to get on my way to Simon's office and see what I can do for him. Thanks for the chat and information, Marko, it's much appreciated. I'll be in touch."

"No problem, glad to help. Be safe amigo.", Marko replied

I left a twenty on the bar, nodded to the bartender and walked out the door.

4

I parked my bike in the garage at the Southeast Financial Center building with 10 minutes to spare. Having only seen it from a distance, the building itself was impressive. By the looks of it, I'd guess at least fifty stories high and I heard that it was home to several well-known companies like Goldman Sachs, Merrill Lynch and Wells Fargo, just to name a few. I assumed Simon was well off to keep that kind of company. The monthly rent alone was probably more than I make in a year. Hopefully that will mean a nice payday for me.

The night security guard was the only person in the lobby tonight. As I walked through the lobby towards him, he turned down the volume on the small TV on his desk and greeted me.

"Good evening, sir. Is there something I can help you with tonight?"

"Hi. Yes, there is. I have a meeting with Simon Dubois from NouveauFusion. Could you tell me which floor he is on?", I asked.

"Let me see, NouveauFusion. Ah, yeah, here it is. They are on floor twenty-three. The elevator is straight ahead", the night guard said with a thick New York accent as he motioned with his hand towards the elevator.

"Thank you", I replied. "Is that the Marlins game you have on?"

"Yeah, the bums are losing again. Down four to the Dodgers in the 5th inning", the security guard said as he reached over and turned the sound back on.

"Like always, right? They need to get rid of that bum of an owner", I said.

"Yeah, ain't that the truth. A new manager wouldn't hurt none either", he said with a scowl.

I thanked the security guard again and walked across the marble floor to the elevator and pushed the up button. The door opened right away. I stepped inside and searched the panel for the button for the twenty-third floor, pressed it and felt the elevator jerk into motion.

A minute later the doors opened into a marble entry-way. Smooth jazz played from the speakers in the ceiling and every sound echoed down the empty hallway. The hallow sound reminded me of walking through an abandoned building and I felt oddly out of place.

Walking down this hallway, I felt like I should be wearing a suit and tie again and talking about my summer vacation plans on some swanky island in the Caribbean.

I spotted a floor directory on the wall and I scanned the listing of tenants on the floor. NouveauFusion was in suite three hundred, down the hall and to the right according to the sign.

Each footstep echoed louder than the last as I walked down the hall towards my destination. When I finally reached the door, I found it propped open slightly with a book and a yellow sticky note on the door, which said:

"Mr. Cole, I left the door open for you as I'm the only one here this evening. Come in, turn left after the reception desk and my office is at the end of the hall."

I followed the instructions on the note and when I found Simon's office door, I knocked a few times.

No answer.

I knocked again and said in a loud voice, "Mr. Dubois, it's Connor Cole."

I waited a few seconds, still no answer.

I turned the handle on the door to see if it was unlocked. It fully turned and I slowly pushed the door open to the sound of a squeaky hinge. I called out again as I stuck my head inside:

"Hello? Mr. – ", I began and then stopped mid-sentence.

Simon's office looked like a fraternity house the day after a party. Chairs were overturned, pictures once hanging on the walls were now broken and shattered on the floor. Papers and a laptop, once on the desk, were now scattered across the floor. Then something brown caught my eye sticking out from behind the desk.

I slowly inched closer for a better look.

"That looks like the bottom of a dress shoe", I thought to myself, now fearing the worst. As I turned the corner of the desk, I saw it was a shoe and attached to that shoe was the body of a man lying in a pool of his own blood!

I looked at his face, which was now ghostly white, and stood there for a second imagining what happened to him and the pain of his final moments.

I snapped out of it and bent down to check for a pulse but found none. A quick scan of the body revealed three bullet holes in the chest, all close-range judging by the burn marks on his shirt, and a dark bruise on the side of his now pale face.

"I hope he put up a good fight before finally meeting his end", I thought to myself.

I picked up a small picture frame from the floor and turned it over. The dead man and a woman were posed on a beach, South Beach by the looks of it, both smiling and enjoying the moment.

"Safe bet this is Simon and his wife or girlfriend", I said out loud as I put the picture back on the floor where I had found it.

I took out handkerchief from my pocket and reached into the man's back pocket, pulling out his wallet. Flipping it open, I compared the id picture to the dead man's face. I felt a chill run through me as it confirmed that this, was indeed, Simon Dubois.

I placed the wallet back where I had found it and thoughts started racing through my mind.

Marko had warned me that there might be some friction between different groups of transhumanists.

Could that have been what happened here? Maybe someone was opposed to whatever Simon was working on? Or, if this new tech is as revolutionary as Marko said, maybe it's worth a fortune to someone, I thought to myself.

I stepped out from behind the desk and stood by the large window that looked out over downtown Miami. The city was lit up and I watched the light trails of cars speeding by on the highway for a few seconds. I took my phone out of my pocket, unlocked the screen and started to dial 911 when I heard movement behind me! I instinctively dropped my phone and swung around to defend myself.

But it was too late.

As I turned, I felt a heavy object strike the side of my head. My legs buckled and I felt myself falling to my knees. And then, everything went black.

5

I woke up with a throbbing pain in the back of my head. Slightly confused I started to open my eyes, trying to remember where I was, and more importantly, what had happened.

As my vision came into focus, I saw one of Miami's finest standing over me pointing a gun at my head. There's nothing quite like waking up to the barrel of a gun in your face.

"Don't move!", the officer shouted. "Sir, he's awake!"

"Turn over on your stomach and put your hands behind your back! Now!", the officer screamed.

His words sounded like cannon fire to my throbbing head.

Not wanting a bullet in my already pounding head, I did as he commanded. As I did, I noticed a gun lying beside me and watched the officer kick it out of my reach.

The officer stuck his knee into the center of my back, handcuffed me and then helped me to sit up.

"Wha-, what is happening?", I managed to say, still a bit groggy.

The officers looked at me, then at the gun.

"It looks to us like you shot and killed the white male behind the desk. We found you unconscious with a gun in your hand when we arrived a minute ago."

"But, that's not my gun! I was here for a meeting with Simon!", I protested.

The cop shot me a disbelieving stare.

"Then why was the gun in your hand?", he asked.

I must admit that I didn't have an answer for that.

"I'm telling the truth; I was here for a meeting. I don't even own a gun!", I tried explaining.

"You and Detective Smith can sort that out", the cop replied unsympathetically.

A few minutes later, which seemed like an eternity with my aching head, a tired looking man in a suit approached me.

"I'm Detective Smith. What's your name?"

"Cole. Connor Cole", I said.

"Cole, here's the situation. We got an anonymous call about a gunshot here. When we arrived, we found you unconscious and the man on the floor over there dead, with 3 bullet holes in his chest. All three at very close range. There was also a gun in your hand. What do you know about that?", the detective asked accusingly.

"Look, detective, I'm innocent. I had a meeting scheduled at 9pm tonight with Simon, that's the dead guy over there", I said gesturing towards Simon, "when I arrived, I found him already dead. The last thing I remember was hearing someone behind me and then getting hit on the head. The next thing I see is Barney Fife over there sticking a gun in my face."

The detective interrupted, "It's a little late for a business meeting. What was the meeting about?"

I shook my head a couple of times to help me think straight.

"The company had a break-in a while back. Your boys investigated but weren't any help. So, I was referred to Simon", I said.

"Why where you referred? What is it that you do? And who referred you?", asked the detective.

"I'm a private investigator. I occasionally work with the local FBI office helping them out on cases that match my skill set. Special Agent Matthew Banks is the one that referred me."

I blinked a few times, still groggy, trying to remember what I wanted to say next.

"Simon is an acquaintance of his, he thought I could help by looking into the break-in. I was here to get more information and to find out what exactly he wanted me to do", I explained.

The detective's face grew annoyed.

"The FBI?", he said unbelievingly.

"OK, Cole, this is all very interesting but I'm sure you know we'll have to check it out and verify what you're telling us is true. In the meantime, you'll have to come with us to the station."

Detective Smith motioned to one of his officers.

"Get this evidence bagged and have the weapon sent to ballistics. We'll need to know if it fired the bullets that killed our victim", Detective Smith said.

"As I'm sure you know we're going to check the gun for fingerprints, yours are definitely on it, which isn't good for you. We're also going to check you for gunshot residue. If that comes up clean, that will be good for you. If not, well, you get the picture."

The detective signaled to two uniforms and motioned for them to help me up.

"Cole, these two men are going to walk you downstairs and put you in a squad car. I'll met up with you later at the station and we can go over your story again, and this time, in more detail", the detective said looking me in the eye, as his men pulled me to my feet.

As I was helped up, the room started to spin, and I felt sick to my stomach. The two officers started to escort me out of the room, and I stumbled, the officers catching me before I could fall.

"You OK?", asked one of the uniforms.

"I'm a little dizzy, that knock on the head must have been worse than I thought", I said.

I stood there for a few seconds, staring at the floor and waited for the room to stop spinning. When it did, I nodded to the officers and we continued our march toward the door.

"You might want to get that head looked at, sounds like a concussion to me", one of the uniforms said.

I nodded and gave a grunt, not feeling like speaking.

I glanced back at Simon, still laying on the floor, as we walked out of the door.

Was the killer still in the room when I found Simon? And who called the police? There was nobody else on this floor, that I saw, who could have heard the shot.

Did someone want me to take the blame for the murder?

A couple of minutes later the elevator doors opened into the lobby. The security guard that I had talked to earlier was watching wide-eyed as I was escorted through the lobby. My current situation obviously more interesting to him than the Marlins game he was watching when I arrived earlier.

Outside I could see news vans and reporters gathered in anticipation.

Getting perp-walked in front of news crews and being seen by the entire south Florida viewing area isn't going to be great for finding new cases, I thought to myself.

The two uniforms led me through the crowd of reporters, some shouting questions, asking what happened and if I did it.

I said nothing and avoided eye contact until we were past them.

When we reached the car, the officers opened the door and helped me inside. A few seconds later the car's engine roared to life and we were moving towards the precinct, and thankfully, away from the watchful eyes of the press.

6

When we arrived at the police station, the two uniforms helped me out of the car and escorted me to a holding room inside the station.

It reminded me of an old episode of Castle, and a small part of me wished Beckett would come through that door to interrogate me. Sadly, I realized I wouldn't be that lucky when Detective Smith walked through the door instead.

"Connor let's start from the beginning. What were you doing in Dr. Dubois's office tonight?", the detective said.

I looked at the detective and sighed.

"Haven't we been over this detective? I've told-" I started, before he cut me off mid-sentence.

"Yes, but we are going over it again. And we are going to go over it in every excruciating detail until I'm satisfied. Do I make myself clear?"

I didn't like the detective's tone but decided it was in my best interest to cooperate with him.

"Look, detective, like I told you, I was there for a meeting with Simon. Agent Banks of the FBI suggested that we meet because of the break-in that Miami PD said wasn't worth their time. He thought I could help figure out who broke in and if they stole any information", I explained somewhat annoyed.

The detective nodded and continued his questioning.

"And you said that when you arrived at the office there was nobody there to let you in, is that correct? And if so, how did you get in?"

"That's correct", I said.

"When I arrived at the office, the door was slightly propped open with a book. There was a sticky note on the door saying there wasn't a receptionist this late and to come in. It had directions telling me which office was Simon's", I tried answering less annoyed this time.

"Connor", the detective looked serious now, "when we arrived there was no book and no sticky note on the door. How do you explain that?", he asked.

"What, I, wait, are you telling me the door wasn't propped open? Are you sure of that?", I asked in disbelief.

"Yes, the officers first on the scene said the door was closed, unlocked but closed. And there was no sticky note found."

The detective paused for a few seconds to let the seriousness set in.

"Do you want to change your story? The time to come clean is right now Connor. If you continue to lie to me, I can't help you", the detective said smugly trying to strong-arm me.

"No, I don't want to change my story! Every goddamned word I have said to you has been exactly what happened. Have you contacted Agent Banks yet?", I asked frustrated, "It seems to me that would be a good idea. He will tell you everything I said is true and we can stop wasting each other's time!"

The detective closed his notebook and looked at me, "We are trying to reach this Agent Banks right now. We should also have the results of the test we did on your hands for gunshot residue soon. I hope for your sake it comes back clean."

The detective got up from his chair and walked across the room, leaving me alone, handcuffed to the table.

I assumed they were still watching and listening through the mirror across the room from me, just waiting for any sign of guilt that they could manipulate.

Sometimes I wonder how I manage to get myself into these situations.

Maybe Marko was right, maybe these cases are more trouble than they are worth. Right now, working for some soulless corporation doesn't sound so bad, I thought to myself.

No! I need to focus on the present, I reminded myself. And right now, the only problems I need to focus on are who the hell knocked me unconscious, why they tried to frame me and why they wanted to kill Simon in the first place.

Twenty minutes later, which felt like an eternity, a familiar face walked through the door.

"Agent Banks!" I said loudly. "You can't believe how happy I am to see you!"

Agent Banks looked at me sternly, like he always does, and said "Connor, I've told the detective that I setup the meeting between you and Simon. They are still waiting on the results from the lab but as long as those are clean, you will be free to go."

"Thanks, Agent Banks. I've been trying to tell them that I had nothing to do with this, but I couldn't get anyone to listen. They were more interested in trying to strong-arm me into confessing", I said.

I continued, "Did they explain what happened?"

"They made me aware of the events of this evening. Based on my experience with such things, it would be a safe bet that Simon was part of something that got him killed. But now isn't the time to speculate about that. I know you've been through a lot tonight, but when you're up to it, I'd like for you to continue investigating. Simon deserves that. If there is anything that I can do to help you, let me know", Agent Banks said.

"Does this mean I'm on the payroll?", I asked.

"Yes. But don't ask where the money comes from, it's strictly off the books. The FBI hasn't been invited to assist with this case so it's not an official FBI case. It's off-book, is that clear?", Agent Banks said seriously.

"That works for me. Besides, I have some payback to give to whoever set me up", I said angrily.

As Agent Banks and I finished our conversation, Detective Smith walked in holding a stack of papers.

"Good news Connor, the lab results were clean. No gunshot residue was found on your person, meaning you couldn't have been the shooter."

"The bad news for us is the gun we found at the scene wasn't the murder weapon either and no other prints were found, unfortunately. You're sure it doesn't belong to you?", the detective asked accusingly.

"I'm sure detective", I answered.

The detective took a deep breath and looked up from his papers.

"Why do I have a feeling you are going to be a problem for us Cole?"

Agent Banks gave a quick, judgmental laugh, confirming his agreement.

"Well, if someone really did try to frame you, they did a really poor job of it. You're free to go, Connor", the detective said as he sat a plastic bag full of my belongings onto the table.

"But don't leave town in case we have more questions."

I nodded, "Thanks, Detective", I said, as he took a key from his pocket and unlocked my handcuffs.

I rubbed my wrists as I stood and picked up the bag, checking that everything was there.

"Connor, I trust you and Agent Banks can find your own way out of the station?", Detective Smith asked.

"Yeah, I think we can manage", I answered as we headed for the exit.

"Oh, and Connor", the detective said, "stay away from this case. Let the pros handle this one."

"Sure detective", I said as Agent Banks and I walked away.

7

I reached into my bag as I walked out of the station and took out my phone.

As the screen illuminated, I saw I had seven missed calls and ten texts. All were from Sophia. I tapped the screen and the phone dialed her number.

"Connor! Finally! Are you OK? Where are you?", Sophia asked worriedly.

"Yeah, I'm OK. It's been a difficult night though. I went to meet with Simon and found him dead, shot in the chest", I paused for a second so Sophia could let all that register.

"When I was about to call the police, someone hit me from behind and knocked me out cold. The next thing I know, I wake up and see the Miami PD pointing a gun at my face and assuming I was the murderer", I explained.

"Any idea who killed Simon and who hit you?", Sophia asked with concern in her voice.

"No, I don't. At least not yet. Agent Banks vouched for me tonight with Miami PD and asked me to continue investigating off the books", I said.

"I could use some help guapa. I need to look around Simon's office and see what I can find on his computers, paperwork, that kind of thing, but Miami PD will never let me near the building, much less Simon's office."

"You're about to ask me to do something illegal, aren't you?", Sophia said.

I could almost hear the smile on her face.

"You know me well. Are you up for some breaking and entering?", I asked.

"Always, like you even have to ask papi", Sophia agreed.

"Let's talk when I get home. I'm headed there now", I suggested.

"Deal see you soon", Sophia replied.

Twenty minutes later I arrived at home and walked through the front door. Sophia greeted me with a huge hug as I walked in. She had a huge smile and was close to tears.

"I'm glad you are OK, papi", Sophia said in a soft voice.

"Me too. I'm OK, don't worry, nothing is going to happen to me", I said, trying to reassure her.

"So, what's your plan for breaking into Simon's office?", Sophia asked me eagerly and wanting to change the subject.

"You aren't going to like it. How's your fear of heights?", I asked, already knowing the answer.

"I still don't like heights, that hasn't changed. Why? What are you thinking?", Sophia asked looking worried.

"We won't be able to go in through the front lobby, I would be recognized in a second. The security guard knows my face and if there are any Miami PD there, which there probably will be, we won't be able to get past them either. So, that leaves the roof entrance and using the stairway to work our way down to the twenty-third floor", I said.

"And how exactly will we get on the roof?", Sophia interrupted.

"Marko has a pilot's license, so I was thinking -", Sophia stopped me mid-sentence.

"Oh, hell no! I'm not parachuting onto the roof of a skyscraper!", Sophia yelled.

"It's easy, amor. We've parachuted before. It will be a piece of cake", I said.

"Yeah, we have, but our landing spot was a wide-open field. Not a tiny damn roof in the middle of downtown Miami!", Sophia's voice now rising with concern.

"We can do it. It's the same, just concentrate on the landing area and there's nothing to it", I tried to persuade her.

"I'm not agreeing to this but let's say we manage to land on the roof. There is still the little matter of the roof top door being locked. But, let's say that I can pick the lock on the roof door and we do manage to get into the stairwell. I'm willing to bet that every floor entrance is protected by a card reader. We don't have a swipe card for access. How exactly do you think are we going to manage to get around that?", Sophia asked, figuring she had stumped me.

"Don't worry, I have a plan for that too."

"So, are you in?", I asked smiling.

"Mierda. This might be your dumbest idea yet Connor. If you are going to do it, I need to be there to say I told you so when it blows up in your face", Sophia said.

"That's the spirit!", I said with a laugh.

The next morning, I made a call to Marko to update him on what had happened in the past twenty-four hours.

"Tio, you want to do what?!", Marko asked disbelievingly.

"Yeah, that's the plan. To parachute onto the roof of the Southeast Financial Center building, after dark, and get in through the roof entrance", I said.

"You are a crazy man, you know that, right Connor?", Marko said bluntly, "And you know what, I dig that about you! Hell yeah, I'm in!"

I smiled and said, "There's one other thing."

"Isn't there always? What do you else do you need?", Marko asked.

"Every floor has a card reader, which we won't have access to. I need a way to bypass the lock. Can you arrange that?", I asked, hoping for the best.

There was silence on the line.

"Yeah. Yeah, I think I can. But it's going to cost you. I know someone that can get cloned key cards. I'll probably need a couple of days to arrange it all. That work for you?", Marko asked.

"Yeah, I can work with that. Let me know when it's all ready and what it's going to cost me", I replied.

"Will do, brother." Marko said as he hung up.

8

The next morning, I woke to the unpleasant sound of my phone ringing and an annoying buzzing caused by the phone vibrating on the nightstand. I rolled over and looked at the screen to see who was calling.

"Good morning, Marko", I said in a gravelly voice, still half asleep, "I hope you have some good news for me."

"Good morning to you too sunshine. And yes, I do. Well, good and bad."

"The good news", Marko continued, "is that I talked with one of my, uh, shadier acquittances. She can get you a cloned key card to the building, guaranteed to give you access to every floor in the building. But like I said yesterday, it's going to cost you. That's the bad news. She wants a grand for it", Marko said.

"Maybe I'm still asleep. Did you say a grand?", I asked rubbing the sleep from my eyes as I sat up in bed.

"Yeah, you heard right, a grand", Marko confirmed.

"And she wants it wired into her bank account today, before delivery."

"Are you sure we can trust her? That's a lot of money to send to someone I don't know", I asked hesitantly.

"I've worked with her in the past, I don't have any reason not to trust her", Marko said.

"OK. Text me the bank account number and I'll send the money. When can the card be delivered?", I asked.

"Today. Once she confirms the money is in her account, I'll meet her and get the card. Oh, and one other thing, tonight is new moon so it will be pitch black. There won't be a better time to do this. I took the liberty of getting the plane ready to go for tonight. You ready that soon?", Marko asked.

"Yeah, we'll be ready. Your plane is still at Opa Locka airport, right?", I asked Marko.

"It is. How does midnight sound to you?", Marko asked.

"Midnight works, see you then. Thanks amigo."

"No worries. See you tonight", Marko replied.

~

I opened the back of Sophia's Jeep and started loading the equipment that we needed.

"Papi, you double checked the parachutes, right? They are packed and will work, right?", Sophia asked nervously.

"Yeah, both are good, nothing to worry about. I packed both our laptops and the lock pick set too. This shouldn't be too difficult tonight. A simple in and out", I tried to reassure Sophia.

"Once we are in, what are we looking for exactly?", Sophia asked me.

"Anything that might make someone want to kill Simon. A new product. Documentation about a business partnership that went south, anything out of the ordinary really."

"I also want to get a look at Simon's lab while we are there too. I saw it briefly the night he was murdered. There might be something of interest in there", I said hopefully.

Sophia nodded.

"Anything you want me to do specifically?", she asked.

"I would love to have a back-door into Simon's computer network. Once we get in, see if you can setup a VPN that we can use from home. Then we can go through his records without being rushed", I said.

"That's easy enough. Too bad there wasn't one setup already, we could have avoided this crazy plan", Sophia said, forcing a half-smile.

"Where's the fun in that?", I replied trying to make her feel better.

After I finished loading everything into the Jeep, I closed the door and turned to Sophia.

"All set, ready to do this?", I asked.

"As ready as I'll ever be, let's go", Sophia replied with apprehension in her voice.

Twenty-five minutes later Sophia and I arrived at Opt Locka airport and found Marko waiting for us.

"It's about time tio", Marko said jokingly, "You two ready to go or what?"

"Yeah, let's do it. Anything we need to know before we leave?", I asked.

"Yeah, a couple of things. First, here is your key card", Marko said as he handed it to me.

"And second, after take-off, it will only be about ten minutes before we are over the drop zone. We'll approach the building from northwest to southeast. So, be ready for me to tell you when to jump", Marko instructed.

"And whatever you do, don't hesitate. It's a small landing zone and we'll be past it quickly."

"We'll be ready, don't worry", I said.

The three of us climbed into Marko's old plane and settled in while Marko went through his pre-flight checks.

Minutes later the plane shook violently and grumbled to life.

I saw Sophia tightening her seat belt out of the corner of my eye.

Marko radioed ground control and got permission to taxi to the runway. He released the brake and the plane lurched forward.

"Taxi won't take long, it's a small airport. If you look this way you can see the runway from here", Marko said as he pointed to his right.

ATC crackled again in our headsets.

"Gulfstream G650, cleared to land on runway 30."

As our plane approached the active runway, we were given the "line up and wait" order from ATC.

Marko applied the brakes and our plane came to a rest.

Marko's voice came over our headsets, "Just a short wait, we've got a plane on final approach to our runway. It has to clear the active runway before we can go."

I glanced out of my window and could see the lights on the approaching plane.

"Marko is it normal to have private planes this late at night?", I asked.

"Yeah, it's common. All the Miami airports are busy, planes come and go all hours of the day and night."

We watched as the G650 touched down in front of us and saw smoke come off its rubber tires as they met asphalt.

Once the plane had taxied off the runway, and was out of our sight, the ATC controller's voice crackled again in our headsets.

"Cleared for takeoff. After departure, turn heading 180 degrees and resume own navigation."

Marko read back the instructions from ATC and then gave the plane full throttle. Seconds later we were in the air.

"No turning back now", I thought to myself.

I watched the ground sink beneath us until buildings were half their normal size.

As we hit fifteen-hundred feet, Marko leveled out the airplane and started turning the aircraft as instructed by ATC. The feeling from the steep bank made me a little dizzy.

As the plane rolled out of the turn, Marko's voice sounded through our headsets.

"OK, listen up guys, we are just a few minutes from flying over the drop zone. Head to the back, open the door and get ready. I'll tell you when to jump. Remember, don't hesitate!"

Sophia and I climbed out of our seats and I slid the door open.

The cool, brisk, night air hit us, and it gave me a slight chill. Sophia and I stood at the door waiting for the signal from Marko.

Sophia winked at me, summoning up her courage. I smiled at her reassuringly.

Then we heard Marko shouting: "Go! Go! Go!".

Sophia and I jumped.

9

I landed softly on the center of the roof, noticing the black parachutes were hardly visible against the black night sky. Hopefully since I could barely see it, no one else would notice us either.

I quickly pulled in the parachute so the swirling wind wouldn't drag me across the roof and hid it out of sight. I turned and looked behind me to see where Sophia had landed. She was nowhere in sight.

"Sophia? Can you hear me?", I shouted over the noise of the wind, which was now starting to whip around the roof.

No response.

Then, as I scanned the roof, I thought I heard the faint sound of something dragging across loose stones and concrete.

My eyes darted from side to side trying to find Sophia in the darkness.

There! When I finally spotted her, she was struggling to cut away from her parachute. The swirling wind had grabbed her parachute and was dragging her across the roof! She was desperately clinging to the edge of the building, trying to not be pulled over the side!

I raced across the roof towards her, the wind nearly knocking me over on each step.

"Hold on Sophia, I've got you!", I shouted as I did my best to pull her away from the side of the building.

The wind, now whipping around the roof at full strength, was tugging us against the edge of the building, trying its best to pull us over the side.

Sophia had one hand wrapped around me and the other clinging tightly to the edge of the building. I fumbled through my pockets trying to find my knife.

Suddenly, a strong gust of wind grabbed the parachute again, causing the parachute to drag us only inches from being pulled over the edge!

"Connor, hurry! Hurry! I can't hold on much longer!", Sophia screamed.

With my knife finally in hand, I put the sharp blade against one side of the taut parachute line and starting sawing through it as quickly as I could. As the wind tried it's best to finish us off, the knife blade finally sliced through the line and the parachute's pull on us let up.

I dragged Sophia away from the edge of the building and quickly grabbed the other line, cut it away, freeing Sophia from its clutches.

I watched the parachute fly away into the black, inky night, relieved that we both had survived.

Sophia was trembling as we both fell to the ground exhausted. Both happy to still be alive.

"I'm sorry Sophia, are you OK?", I asked.

"I-I, I'm ok", Sophia said slowly, "I just need to rest for a minute and calm down. I don't know what happened. As soon as my feet touched the roof, a wind gust got under my chute and started dragging me. The next thing I know the edge of the building was coming right at me. I panicked. All I could think about was being pulled over the edge and slamming into the side of the building across the street."

"You're safe now. Take a deep breath and relax", I suggested as I hugged her reassuringly.

The next few minutes passed in silence, which gave me enough time to realize that I nearly got Sophia killed.

"How could I have asked her to do something so stupid", I thought to myself before Sophia interrupted as she stood up.

"Well, are you just going to sit there all night or are we going to break into this building?", Sophia said, surprising me.

"Uh, well...yeah, we are", I said a little dumbfounded.

I watched Sophia take the lock pick set out of her pocket and walk across the roof to the access door.

I got to my feet and followed her. By the time I caught up to her she had already sized up the lock.

"This is a simple lock. It's hard to believe they don't have something more secure on it. It shouldn't take long to get it open", she said.

She took a small flashlight out of her pocket, turned it on and held it with her teeth in order to free her hands to open the lock pick set.

"These should do it", she said confidently as she pulled the right tools out.

A few twists and turns later, we both heard a click and the door swung open.

"Jackpot!", I said.

Sophia looked up at me smiling.

"Now, aren't you glad I came? You would still be here staring at the lock if I hadn't", she teased.

Sophia took a few steps inside, looked back at me and said, "Well, are you coming in or what?"

10

Sophia and I worked our way down the stairwell, watching the large, red painted floor numbers on each wall decrease as we descended. The sounds of our footsteps echoed off the concrete walls and exposed pipes occasionally sounded with unnerving metallic clangs.

Several minutes later we arrived at the floor we were looking for.

"Floor twenty-three, finally", Sophia said. "Now is the moment of truth, let's see if that expensive key card works as advertised."

I took my backpack off and unzipped the side pocket. I reached in and felt around until my fingers touched the plastic key card.

"Well, here goes nothing", I said.

Holding my breath, I swiped it in front of the card reader, hoping for the best.

Half a second later, which felt like an eternity, the reader beeped. We watched the light turn green and then heard the door unlock itself.

I turned the door handle and pulled it open.

"I guess Marko's friend was trustworthy after all", Sophia said relieved.

"Seems like it. Let's get to Simon's office and see what we can find. And then get out of here as soon as possible", I suggested.

We stepped into the hallway and I looked around.

"The NouveauFusion office is this way", I whispered, motioning with my hand towards the door with yellow police tape still surrounding it.

We approached the entrance and I reach out for the door handle, hoping for the best.

"We're in luck, it's not locked."

Pushing the door open I stepped inside, ducking under the police caution tape. Sophia followed closely behind me.

I turned to Sophia and in a quiet voice said, "Simon's personal office is down the hall to the left. See if you can access the company network and what you can find out there. I'd start with his email account. Look for anything out of the ordinary. While you are working on that, I'm going to check out the lab. Let's meet back here in ten minutes, deal?"

"Deal. Be careful", Sophia said.

"You too", I replied.

I walked to the other side of the NouveauFusion office and into the lab area.

Simon's lab occupied the entire back corner of the floor. It's two walls were glass with a door in the middle of one. A lock with a number pad guarded the contents inside.

Looking closely at the number pad, I noticed that several keys were well worn.

"It's probably a safe bet that the combination has never been changed. I hope Simon was predictable", I thought as I tried to guess the combination.

I tapped several number combinations and was greeted with a loud, annoying buzz each time. I tried a few more times with no better luck.

"Damn", I thought to myself, "but at least the walls are glass."

I peered around the workstation and desk areas. Nothing seemed out of the ordinary until I saw what looked like a high-powered microscope, some medical equipment, a small refrigerator and several large servers.

On the work-area next to the servers, there was what appeared to be several tiny chips. As I started to wish that I could get a better view, an idea hit me.

"I can't get to the work-area but maybe I can make the work-area come to me", I thought.

I took off my backpack and took out a small camera with a modest zoom lens. I held the camera up to my eyes and zoomed in on the microscope. The small writing on the side wasn't English. It wasn't French either, as I would have expected since Simon was a native French speaker. Instead, it looked like a Cyrillic language. Russian maybe? I snapped a picture, planning to identify the letters later.

I swung the camera over to the work-area where the microchips were and pressed a button to extend the zoom lens as far out as it would go.

"Damn!", I said out loud as I smacked the glass with my hand.

The chips were just small enough that I couldn't see it well enough to make out any details.

I'd expect the microchips, but the medical equipment and microscope doesn't fit with what I know about Simon and his company. "What the hell were you up to, Simon?", I said out loud to myself.

Having seen everything I could, and disappointed about not getting a closer look, I decided to see if Sophia had found anything interesting. I walked to the other side of the office and found her sitting at Simon's desk.

"Any luck guapa?", I asked hoping for the best.

"Oh, yeah, I'd say so. I started with Simon's email and found several messages from a local guy named Kaden Lux. It was a pretty ugly exchange. Apparently, Simon agreed to deliver something to him, which he either didn't or couldn't finish in time. It was followed by several threats", Sophia explained.

"And when were those from?", I asked excitedly.

"Two days before he was killed."

"That sounds like a good lead to start with", I said. "Did you find anything with Russian writing?"

"Russian? No, nothing like that. Why?", Sophia asked now looking at me.

"I found some equipment in the lab with, what I assume, were Russian letters on written on the side. It seems odd and out of place to me", I said.

"Are you sure it's Russian?"

"Here", I replied, handing the camera to Sophia, "have a look and see what you think."

"Yeah, looks Russian to me too. It does seem oddly out of place", she responded, handing the camera back to me.

"That's exactly what I thought too."

Sophia closed the lid on her laptop and got up from the chair.

"Were you able to setup the back-door into the company network?", I asked.

"Yeah, no problem. We'll be able to remotely access Simon's network for as long as we need. Or, for however long they keep the network up in the office. By the way, I found Simon's research database while I was looking around too. I want to go through that later and in detail. If we can find out what all Simon has been working on, that might give us something else to go on", Sophia answered.

"Agreed. For now, I think it's time to get out of here", I suggested.

"Me too. What's the plan for getting out?", Sophia asked, suddenly realizing that we hadn't talked about it.

"Down the service elevator. We have a little luck; did you notice the janitors cleaning cart as we came in? There is a pair of work overalls and hat that seem like they should just about fit me", I said.

"And what about me?", Sophia asked defensively.

"You won't like it", I said flatly.

"Just tell me."

"The sides of the cart are covered by a thick, yellow plastic sheet that hides the storage area for cleaning supplies. If we take out everything inside of it, you should be just small enough to fit. I'll push you and the cart into the service elevator. Once we reach the ground floor, there is an exit door on the back of the building. Marko will be waiting to pick us up at the end of the alley", I explained.

"Why do I always end up in cramped or uncomfort-able positions in these plans of yours?", Sophia complained grumpily.

I laughed, "I thought you women liked being small and petite, is it my fault that I use that to our advantage?"

Sophia didn't seem amused.

We walked out of Simon's office and found the aban-doned cleaning cart next to the service elevator, right where it had been when we arrived.

I slipped on the janitor overalls, which were too short in the legs and arms, and I pulled the hat down low to hide my face as much as I could.

Sophia and I remove the cleaning supplies, toilet paper and paper towels from inside the cart and then I helped her climb in. As she did, I took out my phone and dialed Marko.

"Hey tio, we're on our way out. You in position?", I asked.

"Yep, ready to rock and roll", Marko replied.

"OK, see you in five."

I pushed the cart into the elevator and tapped the button for the ground floor. Moments later the elevator dinged, and the doors slid open. I tentatively stuck my head out and looked around. Not seeing anyone, I pushed the cart out of the elevator and cringed at what I heard seconds later. Footsteps coming from around the corner! Someone must have heard the elevator!

I looked around for a place to hide but found nothing. The elevator doors had already closed, and the footsteps were growing louder behind us.

Then I heard a shout from behind.

"Hey! You! What are you doing?", a security guard called out.

I froze with fear, debating on what to do. I said nothing as the security guard came closer.

"Hey, I'm talking to you! Put your hands in the air and turn around slowly!", the guard screamed.

I took my hands off the cart and did what I was told. As I turned around slowly, I kept my gaze on the floor so I could hide my face for as long as possible.

When I was fully facing him, my head still pointed at the floor, I saw the guards shoes a couple of steps in front of me. In one quick move I made a fist, lunged forward and swung where I thought his head should be.

My fist collided with the side of his face! The guard stumbled backwards and fell to the ground, not moving. I stepped closer and leaned over him, my heart racing.

"He's out cold", I said to Sophia who was climbing out of the cart.

"Let's get the hell out of here before he wakes up!"

We dashed around the corner and saw the service exit. Sophia hit it at full speed which slung the door open and banged loudly. I followed right on her heels.

We heard the door slam shut behind us as we turned and ran up the alley.

Winded and breathing hard, we slowed to a walking pace and causally turned the corner onto the main street.

"Where is Marko?", Sophia said nervously.

I looked around and finally spotted him. "There!", I said.

Sophia turned to where I was pointing and saw Marko waiting for us with the engine running.

Trying to look calm, we walked towards the car. The time passed like molasses. When we finally reached the car, we got in and I closed the door.

"Go Marko! Go! Go! Go!", I yelled.

11

Marko dropped us off in front of our condo. I thanked him when I got out of the car and we watched him drive off into the darkness of the very early morning.

"Crazy night. I'm still riding the adrenalin rush. Do you feel like doing a little Google stalking on Kaden Lux or are you ready to call it a night?", I asked Sophia.

"After all of that, I could use some sleep. Let me rest for a few hours and then I'll give you a hand."

"Sure, sounds good", I said with a smile as Sophia kissed me and disappeared to the bedroom.

I sat down at the kitchen table, opened my laptop and went to work. It's amazing the things you can find on the internet today. It's a stalkers paradise.

Four hours later I heard the shuffling of feet on the tile floor. Sophia walked into the kitchen rubbing her eyes and yawning.

"You're still up. How goes the stalking?", Sophia asked between yawns.

"Great. Our Mr. Lux is a commercial real estate tycoon. He owns half of the buildings in downtown Miami and has an office of his own in Miami Beach. It's a pretty swanky one by the looks of it. Last year he started expanding his little empire into other big cities. Chicago, New York, Los Angeles, the list goes on."

"Sounds like a nice life he has going", Sophia said as she opened the refrigerator to look for breakfast.

"Interestingly, it seems he has a taste for travel and hunting too. I found several pictures of him online in, I assume, Africa, doing some big game hunting. I saw him posing with a lion and an elephant", I said.

"That's horrible. How can anyone still do that?", Sophia asked, clearly repulsed by the thought.

"Good question but the pictures are good for us. We already knew that he and Simon had a heated email exchange over a bad business deal, which gave us a possible motive", I explained.

"And now we know he is no stranger to weapons", I pointed out.

"The question still is, what was Lux paying Simon to do and would he kill over it? Do you have anything on that yet?", Sophia questioned.

"No, nothing yet. But given that he owns office space and Simon makes a new type of RFID chip, I'm willing to bet those things are related", I replied.

"Seems likely. So, when are we going to talk to Mr. Lux?", Sophia asked.

"I'm going to pay him a visit today. I have a job for you too, if you feel up to it", I said leaving the question hanging.

"You know I do, what do you need?", Sophia answered.

"I want to get a look at the autopsy report. Specifically, the caliber of bullet that killed Simon. Then we will see if Mr. Lux has ever owned a weapon that matches it. Miami PD said the weapon they found at the scene wasn't the murder weapon so maybe we'll get lucky and somehow tie a matching weapon to our Mr. Lux. Anyway, I was hoping you might be able to use your charming personality to get the info from the coroner's office", I said.

"I think I can manage it. I hope he's cute, we'll see how jealous you are", she said with a playful smile.

"You're just mean-spirited, you know, that right?", I pointed out with a laugh.

"You like it", Sophia said with a grin as she left to shower and get dressed.

After a short nap, I woke up to find Sophia had left. I assumed to see what she could find out about the type of gun that killed Simon. I had my usual quick breakfast of bite sized Snickers and a can of Coke, showered and was ready to go meet Kaden Lux.

His office in Miami Beach was a good thirty-minute drive, if not more, from my condo in Doral. Not that I mind, the drive from downtown across the MacAthur Causeway is spectacular. This time of day the sun glimmers off the aqua blue water in Biscayne Bay and I love looking at the massive cruise ships docked at the port. They make me dream of going somewhere I haven't been before or, maybe more accurately, back to the places I had been when my old company was on top of the world and times were good.

Sometimes I think there is more of an escapist in me than I like to admit.

Thirty some minutes later I parked my bike in front of Kaden's building and walked in through the main doors. The lobby was painted in bright, topical colors, decorated with lush green plants and had a warm, welcoming feel. I smiled as I approached the reception desk.

"I know you, don't I?", the receptionist asked a little startled.

"Yeah, I do, I saw you on the news being led out of a building in handcuffs, right?"

"Yeah, you did. But don't worry, I'm a private investigator and an FBI consultant", I said, pulling out my identification to show her.

"That business downtown was simply a misunderstanding that has been sorted out now."

She took my identification to get a better look.

"Well, it certainly looks official enough. What can I do for you FBI consultant Connor Cole?", she asked as she handed the id back to me.

"I'm looking for one of the building tenants, a Mr. Kaden Lux. Could you tell me what floor he is on?", I asked politely since she didn't seem to be the type that I could charm easily.

"Ah, Mr. Lux, yes I know him", she said in a tone that made me wonder. "You will find Mr. Lux on the top floor. He has the entire floor. He's, well, you'll see when you meet him."

I thanked her and made my way to the elevator. After a longer wait than I cared for, the doors slid open and I stepped in.

"Which floor, sir?", the elevator attendant asked.

"Top floor, please", I replied.

A short ride later I stepped out of the elevator and walked up to the secretary who greeted me happily.

"Good morning sir, how can I help you today?", she asked with a toothy smile.

"I'm here to see Mr. Lux, is he in?", I asked while showing her my FBI identification.

"May I ask what it's about?", she inquired.

"I'm interested in asking Mr. Lux a few questions about a case I'm investigating. It shouldn't take much of his time".

She picked up the phone, told the person on the other end that I was here and that I was from the FBI.

It's amazing how fast you get seen after being told the FBI is here to see you. When she hung up, she looked at me and said, "Please, follow me sir."

I did as she asked and was led to an office down the hall. She knocked on the door and we both entered.

I was taken aback when we walked in. It was as if the jungle had regurgitated all over the office. The walls were a dark wood and were lined with rows of mounted animal heads. All were clearly trophies from hunting expeditions from around the world.

Standing in one corner of the office was a full-sized stuffed bear. A Grizzly by the look of it.

The room smelled strongly of cigars and old leather, presumably from the leather furniture that adorned the office. Smoke hung in the air illuminated by sun light pouring in through the windows.

"How ya doin', it's a pleasure to meet ya. I'm Kaden Lux", a mountain of a man, wearing a cowboy hat and a string tie, said in a thick southern accent.

"Hello Mr. Lux, my name is Connor Cole. I'm a consultant with the local FBI office here in Miami. I'd like to ask you a few questions", I said a bit more formal than I usually care to be.

"Why sure, anything to help out you boys from the FBI. Have a seat", Kaden said in a friendly, southern drawl and pointing to a chair.

"Now, what can I do for ya?"

I sat down in one of the leather chairs in front of his desk. As I did, I felt myself sink down into the softest, most comfortable leather I had ever felt. I could stay here all day.

"I understand that you know a man named Simon Dubois, is that right?", I asked.

Kaden's facial expression and tone changed to one slightly more guarded.

"Well, yeah, that's right. He and I did a little business together a while back. Nothin' against the law about that now is there?"

"That depends. Can I ask what type of business you and Simon were involved in?"

"Well now, as you might know, I'm in corporate real estate. I own a lot of these here large buildin's around town. And, not to brag ya know, but I also own a substantial amount in other big cities around this here good ol' USA, too."

I interrupted, "Yes, we're aware of your current business ventures but back to you and Simon", I said, trying to guide him back onto the subject.

"Oh, right, right, you'll have to forgive me. I got the gift of gab ya know. Got it from my daddy, I did", he continued.

"Simon, well now, he's a good ol' boy. Or was. I saw on the news that someone done killed him. Terribly unfortunate. He sure didn't deserve none of that. Me and him, well, as I was tellin' you before, I'm in real estate and Simon, well, he makes them RFID things, you know those fancy little boxes that you need a card to let you through a door? Well, he wanted a contract with me to provide a new fancy type of RFID for all my current and future buildin's. He had this new type of thing that gets implanted just under your skin you know. After that, there's no need to carry a card around. I dunno about you, but I lose those cards all the time so it sorta made sense to me. And well, quite a few companies are asking for these new implantable doohickeys, so I paid him top dollar for that fancy tech of his. I like my buildin's to have the very best of everythin', you know", Kaden explained.

"And how did that contract turn out?", I prodded.

"Well, now, that's where it gets a bit sticky. You see, Simon was late on delivery. He took the money alright, but never did a single thing he promised to do to any of my buildin's."

"That must have made you angry", I prodded a little more.

"Well, hold on there now! Are you accusin' me of somethin' here, son?", he asked defensively.

"No sir. Nobody is accusing you of anything. I'm simply curious how you handled Simon's lack of delivery on what he promised."

"Well, I didn't take too kindly to it. Where I come from, we do what we say we're gonna do. And I reminded him of our agreement and the fact that he hadn't delivered what he said he was gonna", Kaden explained.

"How did you remind him? Did you send an email perhaps?", I questioned.

"Email? Naw, I don't like using those fancy internet machines. My secretary handles anything like that for me. Naw, me and Simon met for lunch where we discussed the situation like men. He agreed to deliver what he had promised within the month. When I left him, he was still livin' and breathin'."

"What day was that, when the two of you had lunch?", I asked.

"Well, now, that I'm afraid was the day he died."

"And you're sure it was lunch and not dinner?", I asked.

"Yes, sir, completely sure."

"Where did you have lunch?", I asked trying to pin him down on details.

"We went to a place not far from here, The Drunken Dragon. It's a Korean barbecue place, them Koreans, man, they sure know how to cook. You ever been? If not, you gotta give that place a try. You tell'em ol' Kaden sent you, they'll take good care of ya.", Kaden said, going slightly off topic again.

"I haven't but I'll keep it in mind. Do you recall about what time you were there?", I asked.

"Well, now, let me have a think on that. I believe we were there around one-thirty in the afternoon. I remember 'cause our waiter told us how busy the twelve o'clock lunch crowd had been and how worn out he was. I felt bad for him and left a sizable tip to make his day a little better."

As Kaden was speaking my phone buzzed. I took it out of my pocket and saw a message from Sophia that said:

"Had good luck with the cute coroner, Simon was killed by three 9mm slugs."

"Mr. Lux, one last -", I started before being interrupted.

"Please, call me Kaden. I hear Mr. Lux and I look around for my daddy, God rest his soul."

"Kaden, do you own a 9mm pistol?", I asked bluntly.

"Naw, not me. I prefer my weapons, let's just say, a bit more man-sized. No pistol that tiny would take down any of these critters I got hangin' on my wall, now would they?", he asked, seeming rather pleased with that.

"No, I suppose they wouldn't. Thank you for your time today."

"No problem at all. And if you need anythin', I always got time for the FBI. You just let good ol' Kaden know, and I'll take care of it", he promised.

"Oh, and here's my card. It's got my number on it, just in case", he added.

Kaden walked me back to the office lobby, shook my hand and I was shown to the elevator. Before I got in, I replied to the text from Sophia:

"Thanks, Kaden says he doesn't own a 9mm but let's verify that. He did admit to meeting with Simon the day he was killed. I heard about a Korean barbecue place out here in Miami Beach. You hungry?"

I pressed send and waited for a response.

"Always, text me the address."

I sent the address, got on the elevator and headed out of the building.

Next stop, see if anyone from The Drunken Dragon can verify that Kaden and Simon were there when he said they were.

12

The Drunken Dragon was a short, ten-minute drive from Kaden's office in Miami Beach. It's a small place, so small in fact, that if you didn't know it was there you would probably miss it. I drove right past it the first time and had to circle the block before spotting my destination sandwiched between a Subway restaurant and a Cricket mobile store.

I pulled into the parking lot, turned off the engine and took my helmet off. As I did, I heard a familiar voice from behind me.

"I didn't know that you liked Korean barbecue, what made you want to come here?", Sophia asked, now standing beside me.

"I've never had it before, but it seems that this place is one of Kaden's favorite restaurants. He says he was here for lunch with Simon on the day he was murdered. I thought maybe someone here might be able to remember them and prove that Kaden was telling me the truth."

I filled Sophia in on the rest of the meeting I had just had with Kaden Lux before we walked into the restaurant.

The inside of the restaurant was much nicer than its plain frontage. The walls were a combination of lacquered wood and stone. Solid wood tabletops and chairs filled the center of the floor with padded booths lining the walls. The bar area featured a solid wood bar top with edges that looked like unfinished, lacquered tree bark and the occasional knot in the wood gave it an irresistible character.

Thick ropes hung down from above the bar, twisted around horizontal wooden beams in the ceiling, with light bulbs at their ends. The place was inviting and cozy. It instantly made me feel like we had left the busy Miami Beach area behind. If the food is anywhere near as good as the atmosphere, I wouldn't mind coming back here.

Sophia and I walked up to the hostess and asked for a table. At this time of day, the restaurant wasn't very busy. There were a few people at the bar and several couples spread around the main dining floor.

Our hostess took us to a corner booth and placed menus in front of us. Letting us know that they had specials today on their house Sake and various dishes. We thanked her as she left.

Our waiter, a bearded man in his late twenties, with tattoos covering both arms, greeted us as the hostess walked away.

"Can I start you all off with something to drink?", he asked.

"I was hoping we might get some information first", I said.

"We are investigating a case for the FBI and were hoping you or someone else might be able to verify that a person was here on a specific day."

"Well, I can try. We get pretty busy and I see a lot of people. Who is it?", the waiter asked.

"Kaden Lux, I have a pic-", I started to explain before being cut off.

"Oh sure, I know Mr. Lux. He's in here all the time, he's one of our regulars, comes in here several times a week. He's quite the character."

"Do you happen to remember the last time he was here?", I asked.

"Sure do, just a couple of days ago. It must have been between one and two in the afternoon. I remember because the lunch rush was terrible that day and Mr.

Lux left me a very generous tip", the waiter confirmed.

"Was he with anyone?", I continued my questioning.

"He was. A smaller gentleman who wore glasses. Had a bit of an accent too, I'd guess French but couldn't swear to it. I never caught his name though", the waiter said.

I took out my phone and showed a picture of Simon to the waiter.

"Is this him?", I asked.

"Sure is."

"How did they seem to you? Did you notice either of them getting angry or arguing?", I continued.

"Kaden? Mad? I couldn't imagine that. He's about the friendliest person I've ever met. I did interrupt them a few times, you know, checking to see if they needed anything. They seemed to be talking about serious business of some sort, but I couldn't say what that was. I wouldn't say either of them was angry though", the waiter said.

"Thanks, that's all we needed to know", I paused before continuing, "I heard that the house Sake is good, what do you recommend eating with it?"

Sophia and I ordered our lunches and as the waiter left, I turned my attention back to the case.

"It seems that Kaden's story checks out so far. He's a little eccentric but my gut is telling me that he's not our killer. Especially over a contract that hasn't been fulfilled on time", I reasoned.

"Let's have another look at those emails you found and verify they are legit. Someone tried to frame me for the murder of Simon, maybe someone decided that Kaden would be convenient to blame too", I said.

Sophia nodded, "And if Kaden was here for lunch with Simon, and not dinner, we still need to find out who Simon had a dinner meeting with that night. That would give us another lead."

"Agreed, let's get on the VPN you setup and see if we can find Simon's calendar. Maybe we'll get lucky and it will have the dinner meeting on it, along with a name and place", I suggested hopefully.

The waiter arrived with our food and sat it down in front of us. I picked up my fork, about to try the marinated rib-eye, when my phone rang. I tapped the answer button and lifted it to my ear.

"Agent Banks, to what do I owe the pleasure?", I asked sarcastically.

"Just wanted to let you know that Miami PD has arrested someone for the murder of Simon. Looks like your services won't be required any more", he said.

"Who did they arrest?", I asked not believing what I just heard.

"A businessman named Kaden Lux. Detective Smith called me about fifteen minutes ago and said they found the murder weapon hidden in a vent in his office in Miami Beach. His fingerprints were found on it", Agent Banks explained.

"I don't believe it. We just talked to him an hour ago, we must have just missed Detective Smith. We are convinced Kaden didn't have anything to do with it. So far, his story completely checks out", I said.

"Sorry Cole looks like you missed something and with the murder weapon found, that wraps it up. Come by my office when you get a chance, I have a check for you, for the trouble you went to on this case", Agent Banks said before disconnecting the call.

"What was that all about?", Sophia asked.

"Banks says that Miami PD just arrested Kaden. They claim to have found the murder weapon hidden in a vent in his office", I said.

"He seemed convinced that it's wrapped up."

"You don't believe it?", Sophia asked.

"I don't. Who hides a murder weapon in their own office and doesn't even wipe off the fingerprints? Something just doesn't add up. After we finish our lunch, you check out those emails and see what you can find about Simon's dinner meeting", I said.

"And what are you going to do?", Sophia asked.

"I'm going to see Kaden."

13

___

An hour later I arrived at Miami Police headquarters in downtown Miami. I asked the Sergeant that greeted me if I could speak with Kaden.

"You his lawyer?"

"No, I'm an FBI consultant", I said showing him my identification.

"Right this way, sir", he said as he led me to the holding area.

The Sergeant led us through a door and pointed towards the cell holding Kaden.

"You have fifteen minutes."

I nodded my understanding to him as he walked out of the holding area. Kaden was laying on a bench, on which he barely fit, in the corner of the cell when I approached.

"Kaden, you awake?", I called out.

Kaden sat up on the bench and looked up to see who it was.

"Connor Cole! Damn good to see you son!", Kaden said more cheerfully than I would have expected.

"Guess you done heard what happened? About the gun, I mean."

"Yeah, I did. Agent Banks called me and said they found the murder weapon hidden in a vent in your office. And with your fingerprints still on it. That doesn't sound good Kaden. What do you know about that?", I asked.

"I ain't never seen that gun before. Couldn't even say how that got into my office. And I sure as hell don't know how my fingerprints got on it", he replied.

"You believe me don't ya Connor? Good ol' Kaden would never kill nobody."

"Based on what we know, I find it hard to believe that you were the killer. But finding the murder weapon with your fingerprints on it, well, that doesn't look good for you Kaden."

I paused, letting the gravity of the situation hang in the air.

"The problem is, so far, I haven't found any motive, other than the business deal that went bad between you and Simon. Is there anything you haven't told me? I can't help you if you aren't completely honest with me. Let's start with where you were the night he was killed."

"Well, there is one thing ya don't know yet. And I'm a little ashamed to admit this. Ya see, the night he was killed, I was, uh, with my girlfriend. Sweet lil' girl that one. I think you'd like her, she's -", Kaden started before I cut him off.

"I seem to remember that you were wearing a wedding ring when we met earlier today, are you telling me that your mistress is your alibi for the murder?", I asked disbelievingly.

"Well, yeah, I guess that is what I'm trying to say", Kaden said not making eye contact and obviously ashamed. Whether it was the lying to me or the cheating on his wife, I wasn't sure.

"But there is a little more to that story. You see, somehow Simon knew that I was seeing a girl on the side. When we met for lunch, I had every intention of cancelin' the contract 'cause of non-delivery and demand that he return my money. In fact, I told Simon exactly that."

Kaden paused, not wanting to finish the story.

"Go on", I prodded.

"Well, ya see, Simon told me that if I did that, my wife would find out about the other woman. A divorce would cost me millions. And, well, he used the only leverage he had over me to convince me to give him another month to make good on our deal. It was the only choice I had", Kaden explained.

"So, Simon was blackmailing you. You realize that is a motive for killing him, don't you?", I asked, already knowing the answer.

"Well, yeah, I do. And I guess that's why I left it out when we were talkin' earlier today. But I didn't think it mattered none 'cause I didn't kill him. I know I wasn't completely honest with you and I'm, well, I'm sorry 'bout that."

"Is there anyone that can confirm you were with your girlfriend? Someone where you two went or a friend maybe?", I asked.

"Well, now, let me see. That night we went out to dinner and had tickets to the Marlins game. She's a big baseball fan and goes to a fair number of games ya know. We even caught a foul ball that night. Must have been the fourth or fifth inning. You ever caught a ball at a game-", Kaden started to ask before I cut him off again to get back on topic.

"Thanks, we'll verify it. If you caught a ball, there's a good chance you were on TV.

"One last thing-", I said before being interrupted by a notification chirp from my phone. I took it out of my pocket and looked at the message from Sophia.

"Checked out the emails from Kaden. The email address is his, but the emails are definitely fake. The message headers are all wrong, there is no doubt they weren't sent by him. Also, got some info on where and who Simon was with the night he was killed. Let's chat when you're free."

I turned off the screen and put the phone back in my pocket.

"Kaden, when we first met, I asked you if you had emailed Simon. When we searched his computer, we found that he had received threatening emails from you. What can you tell me about that?", I asked wanting to see how he reacted.

"What? I didn't - no, I don't know nothin' about that! What I told you before was the truth, I can barely turn on a computer and my secretary handles anything like that for me. And that's the truth!"

"My partner, Sophia, just sent me a text. She said that the emails look faked and that someone might be setting you up to take the blame for Simon's murder. Any idea who might want to do that?", I asked.

"No, not that I can think of."

"Anyone that might feel like you had slighted them in some way? Maybe from another bad business deal or something personal?", I asked.

"I don't think so. I think I'm pretty fair with my business deals. And personally, well, I can't think of anyone that thinks poorly of good ol' Kaden Lux", he said.

"What about your wife? Does she suspect you are cheating on her?", I asked.

"No, I don't think so. She is gone a lot on business you know, she's been out of town this whole week as a matter of fact, but I'd be surprised if she had any idea about it", he said.

"But don't you worry, I'm breakin' it off with the other woman, good ol' Kaden Lux is gonna fly right from now on!"

I nodded in response, not really believing it.

"Does your office have any surveillance systems?", I continued with my questioning.

"Most of the floor doesn't but I do have a hidden camera in my office. I keep a fair amount of money in the safe and well, ya know, better safe than sorry I always say. It's in the mouth of the stuffed Grizzly Bear in the corner of the room. You'd miss it if ya weren't specifically lookin' for it. It covers the whole office from that spot".

As Kaden finished speaking the Sergeant opened the door.

"Time is up guys. And Mr. Cole, Detective Smith would like a word with you. Follow me, please", he said.

$$\sim$$

The Sergeant lead me out of the holding area and to Detective Smith's desk. The detective pointed at the chair and instructed me to sit down.

"Cole, what are you doing here? I thought I had made it clear that we were handling this case."

"I was asked by the FBI to look into it. I'm simply doing what I was asked to do. And you do know that the chances that Kaden actually killed Simon are next to zero, right?", I asked.

The detective looked at me like I was crazy.

"What makes you say that? Not only did we find the murder weapon, but his fingerprints were all over it. That's about as open and shut as it gets."

"Kaden was with his girlfriend at the Marlins game when Simon was killed. Did you know that? He told me they caught a foul ball during the game and I'm betting they were on TV for all to see. And, maybe the most important evidence, we found threatening emails sent to Simon from Kaden. We've now discovered that they were faked. My guess is they were sent by someone trying to frame him for the murder", I said.

"And why would someone want to do that?", the detective asked skeptically.

I decided not to reveal that Kaden was being blackmailed by Simon.

"Perhaps convenience. They tried to frame me, and poorly, I might add. Since that failed, it's conceivable that they needed another scapegoat. If someone had knowledge that the business deal between Kaden and Simon went south, that would be an easy situation to take advantage of", I replied.

"Maybe. I'll need proof that the emails were faked. That would provide some doubt for his case. And I'll have one of our guys verify that Kaden was where he said he was during the time of the murder", the detective said.

"If he was there, and the emails prove to be fake, that would be enough to get the charges dropped and him released."

"I'll have Sophia send you what we have on the emails. Your tech guys should be able to verify they are fakes", I said as I took my phone out to text Sophia the request.

"Oh, and detective, Kaden told me that he has a small hidden camera in his office. There might be something useful on that footage. It's hidden in the stuffed Grizzly Bear's mouth", I added.

"We'll look into that tomorrow. And Cole, I can't stop you from looking into this case but remember this is Miami PD's case. Try to stay out of our way", the detective said arrogantly.

I nodded but had no intention of staying out of the way.

As I walked out of the station, I took my phone out and dialed Sophia, curious to see where and who Simon was with right before he was killed.

14

"Buenas noches amor mio", Sophia said when she answered the phone. "How was the meeting with Kaden?"

"Interesting. Our Mr. Lux is far from a saint. It turns out that he wasn't completely honest with us. Shocking, right?", I said sarcastically.,

"He now says that his alibi is, get this, his mistress. They were at the Marlins game during our kill window."

Sophia laughed and asked, "Have you been able to verify that's the truth?"

"No, not yet. But he did say they caught a foul ball in the fourth or fifth inning. We can re-play the game on MLB.TV and see if the cameras saw him. I'm willing to bet they were on TV when they caught it. He would stick out like a sore thumb just about anywhere. Anyway, that and the fake emails should be enough to get Kaden released."

"Oh, he also told me that his office space doesn't have a surveillance system but his main office, where they found the gun hidden in a vent, has a hidden camera. I'm headed there now to see what is on it."

"Did you tell the police about the camera?", Sophia asked.

"I did. They are going to send someone tomorrow. That's why I want to see what's on it tonight. I'm not too trusting of Detective Smith yet. You said you had some news, what did you find?"

"I was able to get part of Simon's calendar. It has an entry for a meeting prior to the one with you, it was with a guy named Toby Joss. Google says he's a local venture capitalist and has an impressive list of companies that he's worked with."

"Great work. Let's plan to pay him a visit tomorrow and see if we can find out why Simon would need to meet with a money man. In the meantime, see if you can find video of Kaden at the Marlins game. If you do, send that over to Detective Smith so we can get Kaden out of jail. In the meantime, I'll see if I can find that hidden camera in Kaden's office. I'll be home after I check out the video", I said.

"OK, see you soon", Sophia said as I pressed the end call button on my phone.

~

I walked into the lobby of Kaden's building and took the elevator up to his office on the top floor. The floor was quiet at this time of night, except for the sound of a flickering light bulb coming from the ceiling above me.

As I approached the door, I took the pass card Marko had given me out of my backpack and swiped it in front of the card reader, hoping for the best.

A second later, with a loud beep that echoed through the empty hallway, the card reader changed to a green light and I heard the door unlock. I opened the door and walked through the reception area to Kaden's office.

The room still had crime scene tape around the door frame that I pushed aside as I entered.

On one side of the room, there were evidence markers in front of a vent, which I assumed was where they found the supposed murder weapon.

The Grizzly Bear was still standing in the corner of the office, its mouth pointing diagonally across the room towards Kaden's desk.

I wondered where the safe was that Kaden mentioned to me earlier but right now, I wasn't too interested in finding out.

The camera location couldn't have been better. Assuming it was still there, it would give a complete view of the room. I assumed the stuffed Grizzly was placed there for that exact reason. If someone planted the gun, the video should have recorded the whole thing.

I walked hopefully across the room towards the giant stuffed bear.

The streetlights shining through the large windows of the office gave off enough light for me to see where I was going, but the bear was in more darkness than the rest of the room. Not wanting to risk turning on the lights, I took out a small flashlight from my bag and shined the light into the bear's mouth.

"Right where Kaden said it was", I said out loud to myself.

I reached into the bears mouth and pulled out a small, square, black camera and disconnected it from its power source.

I turned the camera around in my hand until I found the memory card slot and removed it.

Now to put this in my laptop and see what's on it.

I reached into my backpack and took out my laptop. After waiting for it to start up, I inserted the memory card and a couple of seconds later, I was browsing through video clips.

I sat on the floor of the dark room and watched the videos, playing in fast forward mode, of Kaden sitting at his desk answering phone calls and going about his daily work routine until a blond woman entered his office and closed the door as she came in. I slowed down the video to normal speed and watched with interest.

Kaden seemed happy to see her judging by the huge smile on his face.

They sat and talked, about what I couldn't tell, for about 5 minutes before the blond woman got up from her chair and Kaden walked around his desk. The two kissed and as she turned to leave, Kaden lightly smacked her ass playfully. The blond woman seemed to enjoy that, turning and giving him a pleased smile over her shoulder, before opening the door and leaving.

"Dollars to donuts that's the mistress", I thought to myself.

After the blond woman left, I pressed the fast-forward button and watched time tick by at 32x speed. At the end of the day I saw Kaden pack up and, I assume, leave for the day as he turned the lights out and walked out of the office.

Over the next several minutes I saw nothing more than a time lapse of shadows creeping across the floor and then fading into the dim light provided by the streetlights from the Miami Beach neighborhood.

Seconds later, I saw something move in the dark! Or did I?

I pressed the pause button and rewound the video.

Playing in normal speed I looked closer at the screen. I did see someone!

Dressed in all black, a figure walked across the room and to the darkened side wall, the same wall where the murder weapon was found hidden in the vent!

It was hard to see exactly what the dark figure was doing but there is no way this could be a coincidence. I made a mental note of the time index where this happened.

I copied the video clips to my laptop and put the memory card back into the camera for detective Smith's men to find tomorrow. As I stood up to put the camera back into the Grizzly Bear's mouth, I heard the outer office door unlocking, followed by footsteps.

Someone was coming towards Kaden's office!

As fast as I could I put the camera back in its place and shoved my laptop into my backpack. Looking around quickly, the only place to hide was a small closet next to the bear. I dashed inside and quietly shut the door.

Peeking through the crack in the closed door I could half see a person coming towards me with a flashlight, the beam of the flashlight robbing my vision of any details about the person.

Had they heard me?

Wait, no, the person wasn't heading towards me but rather right for the Grizzly Bear!

From my hidden position I could see the dark form of a person reaching to take the camera out of the bears mouth, still too dark to clearly see the persons face.

Whoever it was shoved the camera into their pants pocket and then headed for the exit.

But who else could have known about the camera? Either someone that knew about it has something to hide or somehow, someone else had found out about it.

I waited for ten minutes to make sure the intruder had left.

Not hearing anything else I slowly opened the door, trying to not let it squeak, then made my way out of the office and into the elevator as quietly and as quickly as I could.

A minute later the elevator dinged right before the door slid open to the first-floor lobby.

I breathed a sigh of relief as I made my way to the front door and out onto the street. I waited for the light to signal it was safe for me to cross the street and when it did, I walked into a Starbucks to use their free wi-fi.

I ordered a latte and then found an empty table next to the window.

Powering on my laptop I started uploading the video clips to the cloud. When they finished, I sent the link to Detective Smith, along with an account of what happened at Kaden's office tonight. This will be a nice surprise for him first thing in the morning.

As I walked out of Starbucks towards my bike, I took out my phone and dialed Sophia. She picked up on the second ring.

"It's about time papi, where are you?"

"I'm on my way home, it's been a long and interesting night. I'll fill you in when I get there. Any luck with finding Kaden on the Marlins broadcast of the game?" I asked.

"Yep, he was exactly where he said he was. I sent a video clip to Detective Smith less than an hour ago", Sophia answered.

"That's great news, Kaden will be happy to be released. OK, I'm heading home, see you in twenty", I said as I started up my bike and drove off into the night.

15

The next morning, I woke up to the sound of my phone ringing. Again. I really must start remembering to turn it off at night.

I glanced at the clock and saw it said six o'clock in the morning, an ungodly hour that nobody should be awake to see. I didn't recognize the number when I picked up my phone but answered it anyway.

"Hello?", I said in a gravelly, half-asleep voice.

"Connor? This here is Kaden. Kaden Lux. Did I wake ya?", the voice on the other end asked eagerly.

"It's OK, I'm awake. What can I do for you Kaden?", I asked slightly annoyed at the early wake-up call.

"Do for me? Naw son, you done enough for ol' Kaden. I called to thank ya. They told me this mornin' that you cleared my good name and well, I wanted you to know how grateful I am. Ya know, I need to repay you somehow. How about-", he started before I jumped in.

"Don't worry about it, I was just doing my job and making sure we get the real killer. Which you aren't. You don't owe me anything."

"Well now, that just don't sit right with me. I got to do something. Wait, I got an idea. Do you have office space for your private investigator business? 'Cause you know good office space, in a good location, would make all the difference for your business", Kaden pointed out.

"We work out of our condo in Doral. It's not huge but it's enough for us", I answered.

"You work outta your condo? That's no-good son. Tell ya what, how 'bout if good ol' Kaden gives you some office space, anywhere you want, free of charge. No rent, no electric bills, no nothin', all for free, for as long as you like. I've got all kinds of buildings around town, big ones, small ones, in between ones, it won't be no problem to find some-thing good for ya. Yeah, this is a great idea! What do you say?", Kaden pressed, eager to find a way to repay me.

"Well, Kaden, I don't know. That just doesn't seem right to me. You really don't need-", I said before he cut me off.

"Nope, I won't take no for an answer. Tell ya what, I'll find you some options and send them over to ya. Yes sir, I'll find you the best darn private investigator office there ever was! OK, I gotta go, I'll be in touch!", Kaden said as he disconnected.

"Wait, Kaden, you don't need, hello? Kaden?", I called out, but it was too late, he was already gone.

"Papi, who was calling so early?", Sophia asked with her eyes still closed and not wanting to be awake yet.

"That was Kaden. Sounds like they released him this morning and told him that it was because of us. Now he wants to repay us. No good deed ever goes unpunished, does it?"

"What does he want to repay us with?", Sophia said, now awake and looking at me with her beautiful dark eyes.

"He says he wants to give us some proper office space for our business, completely free, we wouldn't even need to pay for electricity he says. I told him it wasn't necessary, but he insisted. Before I could tell him no, he hung up."

"Hey, if he wants to give us an office, let him. We could use a real place to work instead of the kitchen table and the living room couch", Sophia suggested,

"And besides, if a client ever comes here it won't exactly look professional."

"Yeah, maybe you have a point, but it just feels wrong. I do like the free part though. With my luck he will find us an office right next to his", I joked before pulling the covers over our heads and pulling Sophia close to me.

I had just dozed off again when my phone rang, waking me up for the second time this morning. I had a sudden feeling that I would be grumpy all day because of it.

I sighed as I rolled over and picked up the phone. Detective Smith. I figured I'd hear from him today.

"Hello Detective, what can I do for you?", I asked.

"Hope I didn't wake you, Connor. I wanted to let you know that I got the video from the Marlins game your partner sent over. We released Kaden a few hours ago."

"Yeah, he called us at the crack of dawn to thank us", I said.

"I also wanted to tell you that I reviewed the video from Kaden's office that you sent over last night too. How did you get in his office? Wait, forget it, I don't want to know. I shouldn't admit this, but I'm glad that you went last night. I never expected someone to steal that camera or that anyone else would even know about it. In fact, I didn't expect there would be anything worth stealing on it. But clearly, I was wrong. Do you have any idea who it might have been that stole the camera?"

"No, I don't. It was too dark to make out a face. The only thing I can tell you is they were about average height but being so dark, I can't say if it was a man or a woman. But whoever it was, was probably involved in the murder. What I can't figure out is how they knew about it in the first place", I replied.

"Agreed and that worries me", the detective said with obvious concern in his voice.

"That brings me to the other thing I wanted to talk to you about. I can understand that this case has become personal to you after someone tried to frame you for the murder. Since it seems that you aren't going to leave this case to us, I propose that we work together. You've proved that you are more than a capable private investigator. I'm not asking for much, only that you keep us up to date with what you've found and what you are doing. We will do the same. Is that acceptable?", Detective Smith asked.

I thought for a second before answering. "Yeah, I can agree to that."

"Glad to hear it. You have my number if you need anything. Are you planning on following up any more leads?", the Detective asked.

I sat up in bed and swung my feet around to the floor. Rubbing my eyes, I let a second pass before I answered, trying to decide if I should trust the detective.

"Yeah, we do have one more lead. Sophia was able to find out that Simon met with a local investor named Toby Joss. We are planning on tracking him down today and seeing what we can find out about Simon's last few of hours before he was killed. Do you know anything about him?"

"No, can't say I do. But I'll get my guys to find out what they can and text you the information. I should have something for you later this morning."

"That would be great detective, thanks."

"Sure thing. And Connor, remember, please don't be a cowboy. Let us help you if you need it."

"Understood. I'll be in touch", I said as I ended the call, not feeling quite as mistrustful of Detective Smith as I did before.

"What was that all about?", Sophia asked.

"It seems we have a new ally. I guess we made a positive impression with Detective Smith."

"Can we trust him?", Sophia asked.

"That's the big question. Time will tell."

We got up, showered and I made breakfast for Sophia and me. Omelets and OJ, which turned out pretty good, much to my surprise. Sophia seemed pleased that I finally bought real food instead of my usual Snickers for breakfast.

As we sat at the kitchen table talking, my phone chirped.

"Looks like Detective Smith got us some information on Toby Joss", I said after looking at my phone.

"Toby Joss is out in Coconut Grove. That address is a block off Bayshore Drive if I remember correctly, near the Yacht club. Nice area."

Sophia nodded her agreement as I pulled out my laptop. I punched the address into Google Maps and a second later we were looking at photos of the office building.

A white, squarish, six floor building with blueish tinted windows surrounded by palm trees. Not a bad place to work by the looks of it.

"It looks like the building is made from white Legos", Sophia said.

I laughed, "Yeah, it kinda does. Let's head out there and see what we can find out from Toby."

I took the last drink of my orange juice and we got up from the table, ready to see what the day would bring.

16

Sophia and I circled the block a few times trying to find a place to park her Jeep that was close to the building in Coconut Grove. Once we did, we both hopped out of the Jeep.

As we walked across the street, I glanced over at Sophia and noticed she was holding back a smile.

"You're thinking that this building really does look like a giant Lego building, aren't you?", I said with a laugh.

She looked at me, grinned, and then burst out laughing.

"It really does though!", she said, now laughing so hard she snorted a couple of times.

We walked side by side across the street and somehow managed to regain our composure as we reached the door to the building lobby. I opened the door for Sophia and followed her in as she crossed the lobby and stopped in front of the list of building occupants.

"Toby Joss. Toby Joss. Ah, here he is. Fifth floor, suite two-hundred", she said as she reached to her left and pressed the elevator button.

As we waited for the elevator to arrive, my phone rang. I reached into my pocket, pulled out my phone and clicked answer.

"Hello?"

"Cole, this is Agent Banks. I was briefed on Simon's murder this morning by the Miami PD. I'm told that you cleared Kaden Lux. I assume you have another lead and were going to fill me in today."

"I've only got a minute, but yes we do, we are just about to meet with that new lead. In a nutshell, Kaden was innocent. We found video evidence that placed him miles from the crime scene. It was another convenient frame up, nothing more. We don't know who framed him yet but we're sure that whoever it was, was involved in the murder", I explained.

"I see. Keep me in the loop from now on, Cole. After you finish with your meeting, lets sync back up and go over details", Agent Banks said as he ended the call without so much as a thanks or a goodbye.

"Agent Banks seems to be in a bad mood this morning", I said to Sophia.

"And that's different from any other day?"

"Yeah, good point", I agreed as I put the phone back into my pocket and watched the door to the elevator slide open.

Sophia and I stepped off the elevator and located suite two hundred. As we walked in, we were greeted with a spectacular view through the window on the opposite side of the floor. Million-dollar yachts bobbed up and down in their slips at the Coral Reef Yacht Club and the sun glimmered off the blue water of Biscayne Bay.

We were snapped out of our dreamy daze when a voice greeted us.

"Hello there folks, how can I help y'all today?", a middle aged receptionist said in a thick southern drawl.

"Good morning. I'm Connor Cole and this is my colleague Sophia. We are consultants with the FBI", I said as I showed her my identification.

"We'd like to speak with Toby Joss."

"Oh, of course, one second please", the receptionist said, clearly flustered, as she walked into an office down the hall.

Almost immediately a middle-aged man, dressed in an expensive looking Italian suit, walked out and greeted us.

"Mr. Cole, I'm Toby Joss. I understand you're with the FBI. What can I help you with today?"

"We'd like to talk to you about Simon Dubois. We understand you recently had a dinner meeting with him", I said.

"I wondered if someone would come by asking about him. Let's talk in my office", Toby suggested.

Sophia and I followed Toby into his office, and he closed the door as we entered.

The smell of coffee surrounded us, no doubt coming from the coffee bar on the far side of the office.

"Please, have a seat", Toby suggested as he pointed to two chairs in front of a large, solid, wood desk.

Toby picked up a box of cigars and offered us one.

"Care for a cigar or perhaps an espresso?"

"Thanks, but we're fine", I said, although I'd really like to have both.

Toby took a cigar from the box, cut the end off and lit it. The smell of smoke from the burning cigar now filling the room.

"Mr. Joss, we understand that you had a dinner meeting with Mr. Dubois the night he was killed", I said plainly, waiting to see his reaction.

"I did. He and I had some business to discuss over dinner."

"What type of business was it exactly?", I prodded, looking for any sign he was uncomfortable or hiding something.

"As you may know, I'm an investor. My job is to look for businesses that have promise or are working on the next big thing but need cash to continue. In exchange, we get a stake in the company and usually a place on the board of directors. Sometimes they work out, sometimes they don't but we try our best to minimize the risk", he said.

"And did you invest in Simon's company?", I asked pointedly.

"Simon approached me a few weeks ago looking to take on new investors. He explained that he was working on a new, exciting RFID technology that many businesses had already expressed interest in using but he needed funding to meet the demand. The dinner that night was about telling him that we wouldn't be investing in his company", Toby explained.

"How did he take the news?"

"He wasn't happy about it. But he understood after I explained our reasons."

"And what were those reasons, Mr. Joss?", I asked.

"Well, normally when we invest in a company it's for large amounts of money. Enough for operating expenses, R&D, and growth for several years, so we do our homework before committing. When my people started digging into Simon's company, we found several things that gave us reasons to pause. Well, more than pause. It was enough to dissuade us from beginning a relationship with him."

"That doesn't answer the question Mr. Joss, what exactly did you find?", I asked, now more curious than ever.

"Simon had a cash flow problem. Simply put, he was nearly broke. The research he was doing was taking longer than expected and was eating up more money than he planned for. The company would only survive for a couple more months, at best, before there would be nothing left to keep the lights on. That's not really that abnormal though. Often, many of the companies that approach us for funding are in a similar situation. Truth be told, we were interested in funding Simon. We felt like his new technology would be profitable for us and his company in the long term. We lost our interest in working with him after our investigator discovered that Simon has a mountain of gambling debts. He owes money to some shady people. I'm not talking about the legitimate gambling establishments like Monte Carlo or Las Vegas, Mr. Cole. Long story short, we didn't feel like Simon was a good fit for us at this time", Toby explained.

"Were any of those shady people Russian, by chance?", I asked.

"I wouldn't be surprised if they were, but I can't say for sure", Toby said.

"Some of the equipment we saw in Simon's office had Russian writing on it. I wonder if he was trying to pay off his debts in other ways besides cash. Did your people mention anything about that?

"Unfortunately, no. To my knowledge our people never learned about anything like that."

"One last question, what time did your meeting with Simon start and end?", I asked.

"I was a little late arriving to meet with Simon, it was around six-fifteen when I got there. He had been there since six. We had drinks and that's when I told him we were passing on the opportunity.

After hearing the news, Simon didn't want to have dinner so after we finished our drinks, we left the restaurant. That would have been around, maybe, quarter to seven and then we went our separate ways."

"Mr. Joss, I'm sure you realize that you were probably the last person to see Simon alive. How would you describe his demeanor? Did he seem nervous or worried?", I asked.

"I wouldn't say nervous or worried, but I would say surprised. I don't think he expected us to know about his personal finances. If he was worried, he hid it well."

"Thank you, Mr. Joss, your information has been helpful", I said as Sophia and I both stood up.

Toby shook both our hands and showed us out.

Sophia and I decided to walk to the Yacht club across the street and go over what we had just heard. We found a place to sit next to the water and gazed out to sea to let our minds clear before turning our attention back to the case.

"It seems our kill window has gotten bigger now. If Toby left Simon at quarter to seven and I found him dead at nine, that gives us over two hours unaccounted for, instead of the original hour or so that we assumed", I said.

Sophia nodded in agreement and said, "The gambling debts surprised me, I didn't see that coming. If Simon was in as much debt as Toby says, he would have been desperate. It's a good bet that he wasn't going to get any new investors to keep his company, or himself, afloat with his gambling debt and addiction. I doubt that a bank or any other legitimate source of cash would touch him either. So, if you were Simon, what would you do?"

"Find a way to get myself out of debt, anyway I could. I think it's a safe bet, no pun intended, that he was going to use Mr. Joss's investment to pay off his gambling debts. When that fell through, I wonder if he decided to work it off. Offer to do something of value for someone, in exchange for canceling the debt? Do whatever he had to do in order to survive", I said, still staring out across the water.

"Exactly what I was thinking too. I think it's likely that Simon got himself killed because of it. But here's what is bothering me. Why would someone that Simon owed money to, kill him? Dead people can't repay a debt", Sophia said.

"Agreed, there is more to this. I think it's time we took a closer look at Simon's financials, there must be a money trail, debt payments, something, to follow."

"That trail might lead to somewhere we don't want to be. The Italian and Russian mobs are big in South Florida, especially the Russian mob. They don't call the Sunny Isles Beach area Little Moscow for nothing", Sophia said plainly.

Now it was my turn to nod in agreement. And with that we both stood up.

Sophia and I walked back to the parking garage and got in her Jeep. As she pulled out of the parking space and onto the highway, I scrolled through the contacts on my phone and dialed Agent Banks, reluctantly doing what he asked me to do earlier. He answered after two rings and I began telling him what we had just found out.

"You think Simon was mixed up with the mob in order to get out of gambling debt and keep his business afloat? Cole, that's ridiculous. Simon and I might not have been best friends, but I knew him well enough to know that he wasn't that stupid", Agent Banks said.

"He was stupid enough to get into gambling debts in the first place", I pointed out. "People tend to make the only decisions they can when they are backed into a corner."

"What is your plan, Cole?", Banks asked annoyed.

"Look for a money trail and see where it leads. We still have access to Simon's office network so we're hopeful that we can find something on it. Financial data, bank wires, something", I explained.

"OK Cole. I'm not going to ask how you got access to his network but call me tomorrow and let me know what you've found", Agent Banks said as he hung up.

"I'm getting really tired of that guy hanging up on me", I said to Sophia.

Sophia looked over at me and smiled.

"I've been craving Lomo Saltado for days and I know a good Peruvian place nearby, Chalán on the Beach. Have you been there?", she asked.

"I haven't but I never say no to Peruvian food. Let's do it", I said.

17

The frontage of Chalán on the Beach reminded me of an Irish bar with its long windows and green façade. Once inside, however, it was completely different.

The walls were painted in bright colors of orange and reds with some yellow and green thrown in occasionally, which reminded me of some very traditional Latin American places that I have visited.

On the walls, traditional Peruvian countryside paintings hung alongside the occasional piece of artwork depicting the Nazca lines. The place smelled fantastic too.

Sophia and I found a table and ten minutes later the waitress had taken our order and arrived with the food.

"How is your ceviche?", I asked Sophia.

"Good, some of the best in Miami I think."

"If you say so, I don't know how anyone can eat raw fish", I said with a smirk, knowing it would provoke a response from Sophia.

"It really is good and it's not exactly raw. The citrus juice sort of cooks the fish. You should try it, it's really good", Sophia suggested, already knowing the answer.

"I can't see that ever happening. You know my rule, if there isn't a flame, it isn't really cooked", I said with a laugh.

"Poor Connor, he doesn't like fish. Come over here and give me a little kiss", Sophia teased as she leaned across the table with puckered lips.

I couldn't help laughing at the sight.

"You can keep your fish breath on your side of the table. I might think about it after you brush your teeth a few dozen times, if you're lucky", I said between laughs as my phone started to ring.

I pulled the phone from my pocket and looked at the screen.

"Guess who?", I said turning my phone towards Sophia so she could see the screen.

"It's our good ol' buddy Kaden. I bet he's done gone and found a way to repay us", I joked in the best southern accent I could manage, now feeling happy and not thinking about everything that had happened in the past few days.

"Answer it and find out", Sophia suggested as she took another bite of her ceviche.

I flipped my phone back around to face me and answered it.

"Hi Kaden, how's it going?"

"Why it's goin' great, thank ya for askin'! And boy I think it's goin' great for you too buddy. Good ol' Kaden has done found a great place for you and your partner to work from. I'd love for y'all to come see it. What y'all doin' right now?", Kaden asked excitedly.

"Well, we're having lunch and afterward we have some work to do on the case", I started to explain, not wanting to go.

"This won't take long, come on by, and then you can get back on that case of yours. What do ya say?", Kaden pressed, obviously anxious for us to see what he had found.

"Well, let me ask Sophia", I said, taking the phone away from my ear.

"Kaden wants us to look at some office space he has found for us. He says we'll love it. What do you think?"

"Sure, why not?", Sophia replied with a shrug.

"OK, Kaden. When and where?"

"Well, right now. I'm already here so whenever y'all can get here is good. I'll text y'all the address. I think I can remember how to do that. You know how I am with all these fancy newfangled gadgets", Kaden said, not inspiring confidence.

"OK, we'll wait for the text. See you soon Kaden", I said hopefully, as I ended the call and placed the phone on the table.

"A text? Can he do that?", Sophia asked surprised.

"I guess we'll find out", I said I as went back to finishing my Lomo Saltado and Inca Kola.

As I took the last bite, my phone chirped. Sophia grabbed it from the table and looked at the screen.

"Hey, good ol' Kaden can text after all. How about that?", Sophia said amused, "Let's go see our new place!"

"Are you sure this is the place?", I asked Sophia when we arrived at the address in Miami Beach.

"Yeah, I just double checked it and this is what the text said. That's also where the GPS says we are", Sophia reasoned.

"This place looks more like two houses joined together with a covered walkway between them than it does an office", I said still not believing we were at the right location.

"Let's get out and see if Kaden is here. Then we'll know", Sophia suggested.

Sophia and I climbed out of the Jeep and as we did, we saw Kaden open the front door of the building.

"Howdy y'all! Glad you could make it. What do you think of the place?", Kaden asked in his loud, booming, southern voice.

"It's beautiful!", Sophia said excitedly.

"This is really for us, Kaden?", I asked.

"Absolutely. I got this here office space in a deal I made a few months back. I bet you thought it wasn't office space, I sure didn't the first time I saw it. The guy that owned it was retiring and looking to sell off most of his properties. This one here is the only building he owned that wasn't a more traditional type office building. It's actually two buildings connected together, if ya didn't notice, but yours is this one here on the left. And both floors are yours too. Ya know, this used to be a private house that some folks lived in back when it was originally built in 1934, can y'all believe that? It's been fully restored and is in what they call the Mediterranean style. Plenty of pretty purple flowers and shrubs on the outside too, the curb appeal is great, ain't it?"

Sophia nodded and was smiling ear to ear.

"Anyway, follow me in and let me tell you a little more about this here place", Kaden said as he motioned with his hand for us to follow him inside.

"Like I said, it's been fully restored. We're standing in the lounge, a common space that maybe y'all can use for meetings or for receiving clients. And over this way, there is a private office. It used to be a bedroom before it was restored and renovated, now it's a good-sized office. There's another one just like it on the other side of the common area we were just in, so you both can have your own private office and work area. There is also a small server room on the back-side of this floor for those computers y'all like so much. And ya got a bathroom just down the hall there", Kaden said as he showed us around.

"Now, this whole place is also wired for internet too. They tell me it's got cat6 networking and fast wifi throughout. I dunno what none of that means but they tell me it's a good thang."

I gave a thumbs-up, showing my approval. Kaden smiled, but didn't stop talking, he rarely did.

"It's also wired for something called VOIP tele-phones, I dunno how none of that works either but as long as you can make calls, well, I guess it don't matter none. On the other side of the lounge is a small kitchen. It's got all the basics, small fridge, microwave, sink, and some cabinet space", Kaden paused before starting to speak again, "Well, before we go upstairs, what do y'all think so far?"

"Kaden, we love it, it's fantastic!", Sophia said excited and raced over to give him a huge bear hug.

"Well now, I'm mighty glad you like it little lady.", Kaden said slightly blushing.

"Kaden, this is incredible", I said, "are you sure you want to just give us this? It's nicer than we are used to and I'm sure it's costing you a fortune."

"Nonsense! This property was just thrown in on that deal I was telling y'all about so it's not costing me nothin'. I mostly wanted the other buildin's the guy owned but I had to take this one too or the deal wouldn't get done. Besides, the other buildin', ya know, the one attached on the other side of the walkway, I'll make plenty of rent off that space. Giving y'all this one won't cost me a thing. And besides, I owe y'all for saving my life. It's the least I can do to show y'all my appre-ciation."

"Kaden, I don't know what to say. A thank you doesn't seem like nearly enough but thank you. Sophia and I are beyond grateful", I said.

"There's no need, it's good ol' Kaden's pleasure. Let's go upstairs and have a look around up there."

Kaden led us upstairs and Sophia and I looked at each other, both thinking the same thing: How lucky did we just get?

We reached the top of the stairs and Kaden gave us the complete tour which was nearly a mirror of the downstairs with a couple of former bedrooms turned into offices, a common area and a bathroom with a functioning shower still in it, then he sat down on the couch in the common area.

"Well, what do you all say? Do y'all like it?", Kaden asked.

"Like it?! We love it!", Sophia jumped in.

"It's fantastic Kaden, I'm speechless", I said.

"I'm glad y'all like it. I've got the keys right here", Kaden said as he reached into his pocket and gave one to each of us.

"Y'all can move in anytime y'all want, it's all yours", Kaden said as he stood, and we followed him downstairs.

"If y'all need anything, anything at all, you just give good ol' Kaden a call", he said as he shook our hands and walked out the front door.

~

Sophia and I followed him outside, and we watched Kaden get into his truck. We waved goodbye to him and, as I turned to lock the door on our new office, I noticed Sophia looking at me with a huge smile.

"You realize that we just hit the jackpot, right? No more working in our cramped condo at the kitchen table. We can actually have clients come to our office now. How great is that?", she said, already knowing my answer.

"Yeah, it's amazing", I said as we walked towards the Jeep, "I still can't believe Kaden just gave it to us. I'm anxious to get moved in. This place has so much space we could probably live upstairs!", I said jokingly as we both got into the Jeep.

I started the engine and rolled down the windows as the stereo spring to life. Z92.3 started playing through the speakers and salsa music filled the Jeep before I reached over and turned it down.

Sophia and I spent the next twenty minutes of the drive home talking about our plans for the new office space. After which, I changed the subject.

"So, back to the current case. When we get home, let's see what we can find out about Simon's financials. There must be something in the data on his office computer. Hopefully there is a new lead in there that we can follow."

"I'm willing to bet there is, Simon was under too much pressure for there not to be. I'm still willing to bet that's what got him killed. I could use a hand combing through it all, if you're up for it", Sophia said.

"That works for me", I said as I pulled up to our condo, parked and turned off the engine.

Sophia and I got out, grabbed our backpacks from the back of the Jeep and walked side by side towards the house, both still beaming after seeing our new office space.

When we reached the front door, I took the key from my pocket and unlocked the door. I pushed it open and started to step in when I heard a click. A chill went down my spine. Without thinking I shoved Sophia out of the way and as I started to dive out of the way myself, the condo exploded right in front of me!

18

I slowly opened my eyes, not sure what had happened or where I was. I tried to look around but everywhere I looked was a blur. I blinked a few times trying to clear it away when I heard a voice.

"Connor! Can you hear me?", Sophia asked, muffled.

My ears were ringing but I could understand and nodded in response.

"Nurse! He's awake!", Sophia yelled out before realizing the nurse's station was too far away for her to be heard.

"Sophia, what, what happened?", I asked in a weak voice.

"Connor, the condo exploded. We were coming back from our meeting with Kaden, don't you remember?

You pushed me out of the way, right before it happened. You saved my life", Sophia explained.

"Oh. Right. Right. I do remember now", I said weakly as Sophia started to come into focus.

"I heard some sort of click as I opened the door. I remember trying to dive out of the way after pushing you to the ground. I guess I didn't quite make it in time, huh?", I asked, trying to manage a reassuring smile.

"No, I guess you didn't", Sophia said, touching my hand.

"Where am I?", I asked.

"South Miami Hospital. You've been unconscious since the blast but – ", Sophia began explaining when a doctor walked in and interrupted.

"I'm sorry to interrupt but I wanted to check-in on our patient. Mr. Cole, I'm Dr. Andrews. I've been treating you since you arrived. How are you feeling?", he asked with a serious expression that only doctors can manage.

"I'm a bit groggy and I have a pounding headache. I feel like I have about a thousand cuts and bruises too. Just about everywhere aches. But my vision isn't blurry anymore though so that's a plus. But you tell me doc, how am I?", I asked, hoping for the best.

"Well, Mr. Cole, you are very, very lucky, that's what you are. From what they tell me you dove in front of the brick exterior of your condo just in the nick of time. A second later and you and I wouldn't be here talking about it", the doctor explained before pausing to let what he had just said sink in.

Dr. Andrews continued, "The force of the blast resulted in a concussion and flying debris from the explosion resulted in quite a few cuts and scrapes. You also have a number of contusions, presumably from hitting the ground and possibly the flying debris hitting you as well"

"It sounds like it could have been a lot worse", I said, trying to put a positive spin on it.

"Yeah, it could have. But what concerns me the most is the concussion, so we want to monitor you for the next 24 hours. Any type of brain injury should be treated as a serious injury, so you'll be our guest here for the next day or so. I promise we'll take good care of you. Do you have any questions for me before I leave?"

I began to shake my head and immediately regretted it as I started to feel dizzy.

"No doc, I don't think so", I said as I closed my eyes and waited for everything to stop spinning.

"OK. If you need anything, or you start to feel worse, press the call button on your bed remote, it will call the on-duty nurse. Otherwise, I'll check in on you periodically", Dr. Andrews said as he turned and left the room.

"That sounds like good news", Sophia said now smiling.

I smiled back.

"Yeah, it could have been a whole lot worse from what everyone is telling me", I said.

"Any idea who tried to kill us?", I asked Sophia.

"No, I didn't. As soon as you feel like you are OK, I'm going to see what I can find out. I have no doubt that it's related to the case we're working on. I called Detective Smith and let him know what happened. He's at the scene now", Sophia explained, "If there is anything there, he will find it and let us know."

I heard a knock at the door and looked over.

"Connor, who done whupped your ass this time?", Marko asked laughing.

I managed half a laugh.

"Someone just about did this time, we don't know who it was but we're sure it's related to this case."

"Didn't I tell you that your cases are always more trouble than they are worth amigo?", Marko asked trying to lighten the mood.

"I'm starting to agree with you", I said.

"Marko, I was just telling Connor that I was going to let him rest a bit and go see Detective Smith at the condo and see if he has found anything that might point to who did this. Want to come with me and let Connor try to sleep a bit?", Sophia asked.

"Sure, that's probably a good idea. I just wanted to make sure he was still breathing after his latest near-death experience", Marko chuckled as he said it.

I laughed and gave Marko the finger.

"Try to rest guapo. We'll check on you soon, Sophia said as she and Marko left the room.

"Hey. You awake?", a voice said as I felt someone tapping me on the leg.

I started to come to when I felt another tap on the leg.

"Hey buddy, wake up."

I groaned.

"I'm awake. I'm awake", I said annoyed.

I looked over, expecting to see a nurse. Instead I saw a thin, middle aged man with thinning, slicked back black hair, and a thick gold chain hanging around his neck.

I reached for the bed remote, my thumb hovering over the call button, expecting the worst.

"You Connor Cole?", the man asked in a slight Italian accent.

"Yeah, I am. Who are you?"

"The name's Fat Tony"

I looked him from top to bottom.

"You don't seem so fat. In fact, I'd say you're thin. Are you sure that's your name?", I asked, still annoyed that he had woken me up.

Fat Tony grinned.

"Yeah, I get that a lot. I used to be fat and then I went on that Atkins diet. That shit works great. I lost the weight but not the name. Guess everyone got used to calling me Fat Tony. Whatcha gonna do?", he said gesturing with his hands.

"Well, Fat Tony, what can I do for you? It must be important for you to wake me up after I nearly got blown up today", I said showing my annoyance.

"Well, it's more what I can do for you. It's about what happened to you today", he said.

Fat Tony now had my full attention, as I pressed a button on my bed remote to put the bed in a sitting position.

"Go on", I said.

"You've been looking into the murder of that scientist guy, right? Simon?", Fat Tony asked, already knowing the answer.

"That's right, how do you know about it?"

"Let's just say that I represent some interested parties", Fat Tony explained rather vaguely.

"Who are those interested parties, if I can ask? What do they do?"

"You private investigators, always asking questions. Look smart guy, let's just call it a family business, sanitation mostly, and leave it at that", Fat Tony said.

I stared at Fat Tony for a second.

"Jesus, he's Italian mob. Just my luck", I thought to myself.

"Why is a family sanitation business interested in my investigation of Simon?", I asked, playing along with his cover story.

"Let's just say that we have some competition with another family and their, uh, sanitation business", Fat Tony started to explain.

"Listen, my head is pounding. I'm tired and I'm pissed off that someone tried to kill me today. Let's cut the shit. You're Italian mob, I know it and you know it. Give it to me straight, why are you here?", I said.

Fat Tony laughed.

"I like you Connor. You're straight to the point and you don't take any shit. I respect that", he said before pausing for a few seconds.

"Listen, I have some information for you about the investigation"

"I'm all ears, let's have it", I said.

"As I'm sure you've figured out, Simon was having money problems. Both with his business and personally. That guy had more vices than both of us put together, ya know what I mean? But the one that cost him the most was the gambling. He had a very generous line of credit with a certain illegal, Russian gaming establishment here in South Florida. For such a smart guy, he sure made some stupid decisions. Anyway, he was in deep. So deep that he'd never be able to repay it."

"Yeah, we have already figured that out. What we don't know is why they killed him", I said.

"I'm getting to that", Fat Tony said, a bit annoyed that I interrupted his story.

"Ok, ok, go on then...", I said.

"The Russians knew that Simon was interested in this uh, bio hacking. Crazy shit like altering genes, research on augmenting intelligence, you know, that kinda shit", Fat Tony started to explain.

"Fuck", I said as I sighed out loud. "This is worse than I thought."

"Yeah, fuck just about sums it all up. The Russians offered him a deal; they would forgive his gambling debts in exchange for him doing research for them. We suspect that was pretty much the plan all along. Play on his vices and once he owed them big money, they owned him."

That would explain the equipment I saw in Simon's office with Russian writing on it.

"What kind of research exactly?", I asked.

"We both know that Putin is essentially a dictator in Russia, and he will be until the day he dies. Now, how much do you think research into life extension or augmented intelligence would be worth to him personally or people in his government?", Fat Tony said, trying to lead me to the answer.

"All of that might be true, but it doesn't explain why they killed him. At least, I'm assuming they killed him", I pointed out.

"We don't know for sure if they did but it's a pretty good bet that's what went down. We think that either Simon couldn't deliver what he promised he could and became useless to them or he grew a conscience and told them he wouldn't continue. Either way, it's a good bet that they killed him because of it", he said.

"What makes you so sure?"

"Let's just say that we have people that specialize in keeping us in the know about the competition."

"OK. But why come and tell me all of this?", I asked.

"Well, the sanitation business is very competitive", Fat Tony started before I finished his thought.

"And if I can find Simon's killer, and take him and his partners down, there would be less competition for you in South Florida. Which has the added bonus that you don't have to get your hands dirty", I said.

Fat Tony smiled, "Let's just say that my family wouldn't mind having a monopoly in the sanitation business again, so getting them off our turf would be very beneficial to us."

"It might also be useful for you to know that we think the Russians have someone high ranking in South Florida watching their backs. We don't know who yet but we do know it's someone with some power. If we find out more, we'll be in touch", Fat Tony said.

Fat Tony got up from the chair, getting ready to leave.

"Oh, one more thing. You can bet that since you've stuck your nose into Simon's murder that the Russians are paying close attention to you. I wouldn't be surprised if they have listening devices planted or have people following you. Maybe both", he added.

"Or actively trying to kill me, which would explain the condo exploding", I said.

"That too. Do yourself a favor Cole, check for listening devices. Cars, phones, anywhere that you spend time. And watch your back", he suggested.

"Bit late for watching my back but I'll do my best. If I need anything, or have more questions, how can I reach you?", I asked.

"That your phone on the table?", he asked.

"Here's a phone number, call anytime, day or night, someone will answer", Fat Tony said as I punched the number into my phone.

"We'll help you if we can, within reason. We are just a sanitation company after all", he said with a wink and then walked out of the room.

I watched Fat Tony disappear around the corner and immediately sent a text to Sophia.

"You'll never guess who just came to visit me. I'll fill you in when you're back."

I place the phone back on the table and closed my eyes, hoping for a little uninterrupted sleep.

19

"Time for dinner Mr. Cole", the nurse said as she came into the room holding a tray of hospital food.

The sound of her voice startled me awake. If you need to rest, a hospital is the worst place to do it. Machines beep and grunt every few minutes, nurses checking on you without any regard for if you're awake or sleeping. And of course, in my case, Italian mob guys tapping your foot over and over to see if you're awake.

"Thanks", I said to the nurse, trying to not sound annoyed.

The nurse pulled the food table across the bed and sat my tray on it.

"Enjoy. I'll be back later to pick it up."

The nurse turned to leave, and I took a bite of my food. Bland. I guess there is a reason that nobody likes hospital food. I took another bite and then reached for the bed remote to turn on the TV. When the screen came to life an old episode of Three's Company was playing on TV Land. Jack fell down a time or two, Chrissy was confused, and they all had a misunderstanding. I think I could have written an episode of Three's Company back in the day.

"Knock, knock", a voice came from across the room.

I looked over to the door and saw Sophia.

"You're right in time for dinner guapa, care for some?", I asked

"That depends. Is it any good?", Sophia asked looking at the plate.

"Nope."

"In that case, I'll pass", Sophia said.

I took another bite of peas from my plate.

"So, are you going to keep me in suspense? Who was here?", Sophia asked.

"Italian mob."

"What?!", Sophia yelled out in surprise.

"Yeah, I thought he was here to finish me off at first", I said.

"What was his name? What did he want?"

"Fat Tony. He said he had information about Simon's murder. He claims that the Russian mob was behind it and they were making Simon do research for the Russian government. Oh, and get this, he never came right out and told me that he was Italian mob. He claimed he and his family were in, get ready for this, sanitation. How cliché can you get, right?", I said slightly amused.

Sophia didn't seem amused at all. Not even slightly.

"It actually gets worse", I continued.

Sophia raised an eyebrow in disbelief.

"The information we got about Simon being deep in debt to the wrong people seems to be true. Per Fat Tony, he was in debt to the Russian mob. It seems Simon's gambling vices include illegal gaming, the kind that the mob is fond of running", I explained.

"So, Simon liked underground poker games?", Sophia asked.

"Basically, I didn't ask what he played but it could be poker, who knows."

"So, he was in serious debt to the mob and couldn't pay up? Surely they wouldn't kill him over that. Dead people can't pay", Sophia reasoned.

"Well, you're close. Somehow the Russians knew that Simon was interested in bio hacking. Supposedly, the mob was interested in the technology for mother Russia and I would imagine for themselves too. Fat Tony claims that the Russian mob planned for Simon to get so far in debt with them. And once he did, they would own him and then his research too."

"Dios mio", Sophia said.

"I said fuck when he told me but Dios mio will work too", I said.

"But that still doesn't explain why Simon is dead", Sophia pointed out.

"Yeah, I said the same thing. And Fat Tony didn't have a solid answer for that, but he did say that his people think that either Simon couldn't do what he promised, or he grew a conscience and refused to finish the research, fearing what it might lead to. Whichever it was, it had the same result, Simon murdered."

"Anything else?", Sophia asked.

"Yeah, there is."

Sophia sighed, "OK, what is it?"

"He said that they think the Russians have someone watching out for their activities in South Florida. Someone high up in government or law enforcement would be my guess. He said they don't know who yet. And, this one you really aren't going to like. He said that there is no doubt that we have been, and continue to be, on the Russian's radar. More than likely they've been keeping tabs on us and the investigation."

"That would explain the person that broke into Kaden's office after you copied the surveillance video. And why our condo exploded after we found out about Simon's money problems and were about to look through his financial data. We were getting close to finding another lead. Either someone we talked to is linked to the Russians or they are eavesdropping on us", Sophia said.

"Well, that's another thing I haven't told you yet. Fat Tony said he wouldn't be surprised if they had listening devices or people watching our movements. Maybe both", I said.

"If they have us bugged, it would have to be in the things we have with us all the time. Phones, laptops, maybe the Jeep or your bike. Let me see your phone, where is it?", Sophia said anxiously.

I pointed to the table and Sophia took it out of its case and turned the phone over.

"Look what I just found!"

Sophia pulled a tiny listening device the size of a dime from the back of my phone. After looking it over, she dropped it to the ground and stepped on it.

"I'll take what is left of this and have Marko look it over. Maybe he can give us an idea who made it and where it came from", she said.

"We need to check your phone and the Jeep too. Just in case there are more", I suggested.

Sophia took her phone out of its case and turned it over.

"Nothing here", she said relieved. "I'll give the Jeep a once over too. I'll be right back."

"Wait, you didn't tell me if you had any luck at the condo?", I asked.

"No, Miami PD has the scene taped off and they wouldn't let me through. I hung around for a while hoping to hear something but either they hadn't found anything or wouldn't tell me. Detective Smith promised to call as soon as he had anything."

"Question is, can we trust him now that we think the Russians have someone watching their back?", I pointed out.

"If the Russians really have someone in law enforcement or government looking out for them then that's a good question. I'm not sure who we can trust right now", Sophia replied.

We sat there in silence for a few minutes both pondering what was just said. Then Sophia broke the silence.

"I'm going out to check for bugs in my Jeep. I'll be back soon. You finish your dinner."

With that, Sophia disappeared around the corner and I took the last bites of my bland food.

What I wouldn't give for a Snickers and some Coke right now.

20

SOPHIA

I walked out of Connor's hospital room, took the listening device out of my pocket and held it in the palm of my hand. I snapped a quick picture with my phone and sent it to Marko on WhatsApp. Once I verified it went through, I dialed Marko's number.

"Hola Sophia, can I assume you and Connor need something again? Or did you finally get tired of Connor and want to talk to a real man?", he said in his usual flirty style.

"Oh Marko, if I wanted a real man, I wouldn't have called you. I do need a favor though, something that your expertise can help with."

"I'm hurt Sophia. But OK, what do you need?", Marko asked, his demeanor now changing from joking to somewhat serious.

"Well, quite a bit has happened since you left the hospital earlier today. I just sent you a message on WhatsApp, it's a picture of a listening device that I found on Connor's phone. I found it planted between the back of the phone and the inside of the case. I crushed it so it doesn't work anymore but the serial number is still visible in the photo. We're fairly certain that the Russians have been keeping tabs on, not only us, but the investigation too", I explained.

"That would certainty explain a lot. But how do you know it's the Russians that planted it? And when would someone have the chance to put it there? You know how Connor is, he's practically glued to that phone all day long", Marko asked.

"You're right about that and we don't know for sure how or when someone had the opportunity to plant the device. And we don't know for sure it was the Russians, but Connor had a visit from a guy associated with the Italian mob called Fat Tony. He hinted that the Russians were behind Simon's murder, the stealing of the video from Kaden's office, and our condo exploding that nearly killed us both. I was hoping that you might be able work your magic and see if you can track the serial number on it and find out where it came from and who made it, if possible."

"Will do chica, it will take me a few hours. I'll get back to you as soon as I have something", Marko said, "And Sophia, if there was one listening device, there are probably others. Have you checked your phone, the Jeep, and all your personal property yet?"

"I checked my phone, it was clean. I'm on my way to the parking garage to check the Jeep. It freaks me out that people have been listening in on our lives", I said.

"Yeah, don't blame you there. At least you know about them now. Let me know what you find in the Jeep. If you find one, I'd like to see it before you crush it. It might be able to tell us more if it's intact", Marko suggested.

"I'm hoping there isn't any more but if there is, I'll keep it for you."

"What about this Fat Tony, have you checked him out yet?", Marko asked concerned.

"No, we haven't had time yet. If you want to tackle that too, we'd be grateful", I said.

"Yep, can do, I'll get someone on that while I look into the bug you found. By the way, how is Connor feeling, better now?", Marko asked.

"Yeah, he's improving, I think. He looks better and was eating when I left his room a few minutes ago. We're hopeful that they will release him tomorrow morning. I'm going to tell him that he needs to take a break and take it easy for a few days, but I know he won't want to hear that. He's been solely focused on solving this case, no matter what."

"That sounds like the Connor I know. He's stubborn. When he gets something in his head, he doesn't stop. Do you two have a place to stay? I assume your condo isn't livable anymore", Marko asked.

"The condo is toast. My guess is that it will be torn down and rebuilt. I'm not sure it will be us that rebuilds though, my guess is Connor will sell what's left including the land. In the meantime, we're going to stay in the office that Kaden gave us. It's a nice building in a great location and it looks like we can live there easily. We talked about staying there permanently. Connor likes the idea of living for free. I do too, if I'm honest", I replied.

"I bet, a free place to live in Miami Beach, you two hit the jackpot. OK, if you all need anything, you know how to reach me. I'll get on this listening device and see what I can find from the serial number."

"Thanks Marko. You know how to reach us when you have something", I said.

"No problem. Talk later", Marko said as he ended the call.

～

I made my way from the hospital to the parking garage and found my Jeep parked in the back corner of the first floor, where I left it when I arrived earlier in the day.

I pressed the button on the key remote and heard the Jeep unlock. I opened the driver's side door and started the search for listening devices by looking under the seat, inside the console, each and every cubby hole, cup holder, glove box and even underneath the floor mats. Nothing.

I repeated the search on the front passenger's side with nothing to show for it but a few Snickers wrappers that had found their way under the seat.

"I wish I knew how Connor eats the way he does and stays in such good physical shape. For me, if I just smell chocolate, I end up with five extra pounds that I don't want. Lucky bastard", I thought to myself.

Not finding anything of interest in the front, I closed the passenger side door, walked to the back door and opened it.

As I started the search again, the sound of a tire squealing around a corner startled me. I looked over my shoulder to see an SUV turning the corner and leaving the parking garage.

I sighed with relief.

"With everything that has happened lately, it all has me on edge", I thought to myself.

I turned my attention back to searching the Jeep when I heard a voice coming from behind me.

"Excuse me", the voice said.

It startled me so much that I involuntarily jumped and hit my head on the top of the metal doorframe.

I rubbed the now small, tender knot on the top of my head as I started to turn around to see who it was and what they wanted.

As I turned, I started to panic when I saw a rag coming towards my face!

I was pinned between the attacker and the Jeep! I tried to think quickly about options but there were none. I swung my fists wildly, but it was in vain. I felt the rag hit my face and smelled a slightly sweet chemical smell.

"Chloroform! Son of a -", I thought to myself as I started to lose conscientiousness.

A couple of seconds later everything got fuzzy and then my world went dark.

21

CONNOR

The sound of my phone ringing took my attention away from the TV in the corner of the room. For the first time in several days I felt somewhat relaxed. I picked up the phone and saw it was Marko.

"Hey Marko, what's up amigo?", I asked.

"I'll tell you what's up amigo, I've been working hard for you two. And for no pay I might add. You do know you owe me, right?", Marko said, I assumed half kidding but it's hard to tell with him sometimes.

"Yeah, yeah, I know. I'd offer you some of the Snickers I got in payment from the FBI but they, you know, they blew up with the condo", I said, teasing Marko a little but didn't get any laugh from him, "So, what do you have for us?"

"Sophia called a couple of hours ago and had me trace a listening device that she found. I tried to call her, but she didn't answer", Marko explained.

"Yeah, she said she was going out to check the Jeep, but she hasn't gotten back yet. I assumed she was still out there or got sidetracked. Or maybe there isn't any signal in the parking garage", I said, thinking out loud.

"Yeah, probably not. OK, listen, this is what I found. The device isn't consumer grade so there wasn't a way to track where it was sold. What I did find was that it's military grade. Russian military grade", Marko let that hang in the air for a moment before continuing, "It looks like what Fat Tony told you was correct, at least that part of it."

"I'm not surprised that it's Russian. I guess the plus side to you confirming that it is, is that it gives the rest of Fat Tony's story some validity too", I reasoned.

"Yeah, it does but I'm not sure I'd consider that a plus. It also means that they aren't just keeping tabs on the investigation, it's also clear to me that they are the ones that are trying to kill you", Marko said bluntly.

"Always looking on the dark side, eh Marko?", I said, trying to lighten the mood.

"Just saying the truth."

"I know. And I am worried. That's why I need to get out of this hospital and back on the case. At least then I can be pro-active", I said.

"Your being proactive has gotten you framed for murder and your condo blown up. Not to mention a concussion and almost killed."

"All the more reason to find the sons of bitches behind this and end it", I said.

"Then do it. And let me know if I can help", Marko said.

"Will do. Thanks brother", I said as the call disconnected.

I started to place my phone back on the side table when I heard it chirp. I looked at the screen and saw a text message from an unknown number. I tapped the message to view it:

"Cole, we have Sophia. If you want to see her alive again, come to the cargo warehouses on the west side of Opa Locka airport in one hour. And come alone. Any funny business and she dies."

"Fuck!", I yelled as I jumped out of the hospital bed, ripping off the monitoring equipment that was connected to me.

The room started to spin as I stood up and I felt slightly nauseated. I looked down and steadied myself for a moment by placing my hand on the wall. A few seconds passed and my world stopped spinning, returning to normal.

I ripped off my hospital gown, standing there in my boxer briefs when a nurse rushed into the room, clearly alerted when I disconnected the wires they had attached to me.

"Mr. Cole, what are you doing? You shouldn't be standing", the nurse said with a serious expression on her face.

"Sorry, but it's time for me to check out", I said as I grabbed my clothes from the chair in the corner of the room.

"Mr. Cole, I really must insist that you get back in bed! The doctor hasn't cleared you to leave yet! You could make your condition worse!", she exclaimed.

I ignored the nurse's pleas and finished putting my clothes and shoes on. I grabbed my phone off the table and raced out into the hallway, nearly colliding with an old man walking with a rolling IV pole. He cursed something that I couldn't make out while I spotted the elevator down the hall. I hit the down button several times.

"C'mon! C'mon!", I yelled, hitting the buttons a few more times hoping that would make it arrive more quickly.

It seemed like an eternity passed before the doors opened.

When they did, two orderlies were standing there to greet me. I assumed they were called by my nurse.

"Mr. Cole, it's important that you return to your room. You aren't well enough to -", one started to say before I dashed toward the stairs.

"Sorry guys, gotta go, no time to discuss it!", I yelled over my shoulder as I slammed the door open and ran down the stairs two at a time.

The stairs led to the main lobby of the hospital where I looked from side to side until I saw the exit. A few seconds later and I was standing in bright sunshine. I took a deep breath of fresh Miami air when I remembered my bike wasn't here.

"How the hell am I going to get to Sophia?", I thought to myself.

"The Jeep!", I said out loud as I remembered she drove here and parked in the garage.

I sprinted across the street and entered the first floor of the garage. Running as quickly as I could around the parking area, I finally spotted the Jeep. When I reached it, I saw that the back door was still open, and Sophia's keys and phone lay on the ground.

"They must have jumped her while she was looking for bugs in the Jeep", I said out loud.

I picked up the keys and phone from the cool concrete surface and slammed the back door shut. Racing around to the driver's side I jumped into the front seat and started the engine.

The engine roared to life and I slammed it into reverse. The tires squealed and echoed throughout the parking garage as I stomped the accelerator. The Jeep sprung out of the parking spot and I shifted into drive, speeding out of the garage as fast I could!

22

The drive from South Miami Hospital to Opa Locka airport is normally a thirty-minute drive, I was a mile from the exit off the interstate in fifteen minutes.

As I flew down the interstate, I realized that walking into the warehouse, unarmed and alone, would be a certain death sentence. Not just for Sophia but for me too.

My mind raced, churning through ideas until one hit me. I remembered that I had once attended a funeral at Vista Memorial Gardens and during the service the annoying sounds of private jets and prop planes from Opa Locka airport could be heard buzzing around. I bet if I could get high enough up, I would be able to get a good view of the warehouses at the airport. Then, at least, I'd have an idea of what I was walking into.

"It's worth a shot!", I said to myself.

I swung the Jeep off the interstate and onto Red Road, entering Vista Memorial Gardens on the backside in the hopes that I wouldn't be noticed and that there wouldn't be a funeral going on today.

I drove along the winding road until I reached the far east side. I parked the Jeep beside a tall Oak tree and checked the clock on my phone. Thirty minutes until the deadline.

Sophia always keeps gear in the back of the Jeep and with any luck she will still have a pair of binoculars stashed there. I jumped out of the Jeep and opened the back tailgate, lifted the mat and started digging around in the storage compartment until I saw a black duffel bag with an Adidas logo on it. I unzipped the bag and looked inside.

"Oh, Sophia, that's my girl!", I said in excitement.

Inside was a treasure trove. A pair of high-quality Upland Optics Perception binoculars, several knifes that looked military, a loaded Glock 26 handgun, several changes of clothes, two passports and a few stacks of US dollars and Euros, easily worth a few thousand each.

"This must be Sophia's Go Bag, smart girl, she's always thinking ahead", I thought to myself.

I strapped one of the knives to my lower leg and put the gun in the waist of my pants, covering it with my shirt. Then took the binoculars out of their case and hung them around my neck with the strap.

I held onto the roof of the Jeep as I put one foot on the top of the tire and pulled myself up, then climbing the rest of the way up onto the roof of the Jeep. I grabbed a low branch of the Oak tree that I was parked next to and climbed my way up about twenty feet until I was high enough up to get a good view of the warehouses at Opa Locka airport.

I put the binoculars up to my eyes and looked from warehouse to warehouse and saw...nothing. No movement, no people.

I swung the binoculars back around, slowly scanning each warehouse until I saw something. Two guards making their rounds, both dressed in airport security guard uniforms but with distinctive Russian facial features. It's a safe bet I found the warehouse where they are holding Sophia.

As the guards turned the corner, I pressed start on my phone's stopwatch and then waited for them to return. When they did, I made a note of the time, two minutes and forty-seven seconds to complete a round. If I time it right, I should be able to get a look inside and see what I'm dealing with, without being seen.

I worked my way down the tree and stepped back onto solid ground as I wiped the sweat from my face.

Fifteen minutes left until their deadline.

I locked the Jeep and put the keys back in my pocket. Then I sprinted across the quarter mile between me and the warehouse.

A couple of minutes later, breathing heavily, I reached a shipping container near the warehouses and hid behind it, waiting for the guards to appear again. When they did, I waited for them to disappear around the corner, and I set the timer on my phone for two minutes and forty-seven seconds and pressed start.

I raced towards the front of the building and carefully looked inside through the dirty window.

Inside I saw a wide-open concrete floor, with a work area on the left-hand side and a small office next to it but no people inside. The dirt on the window blocked me from seeing the rest of the interior. I took my hand and rubbed a circle in the dirt so I could see. Then a chill ran down my spine. When I removed my hand from the window, I saw Sophia gagged and tied to a chair in the middle of the warehouse! I felt a rush of adrenalin hit me. I checked my phone, less than one minute until the guards would be back here.

As quietly as I could I opened the heavy door to the warehouse and stepped inside. With nobody else in view, I raced across the room to Sophia. The muffled sounds of Sophia trying to tell me something filled the air as I untied her gag.

"Connor, get out of here! It's a trap!", Sophia screamed.

No sooner than she finished speaking, I heard the heavy metal door slam shut and the unmistakable sound of the door being locked from the outside!

The sound of boots walking across a metal walkway above echoed in the mostly empty room. Then, two guards came running down a hallway towards us, pointing semi-automatic weapons in our direction. I slowly started to reach for the gun under my shirt.

"I wouldn't do that if I were you Mr. Cole", a familiar voice with a slight Russian accent said from the walkway above me.

I looked up to see who it was.

I stood there, mouth open, unable to say a word.

23

"Agent Banks?!", I said dumbfounded.

"Why are you? How? What is going on?", I asked unable to form a coherent sentence.

"Cole, I think you have already figured it out. You just aren't accepting what you are seeing. I'm Russian. I've been a Russian plant for decades. When I was sent here, my mission was to infiltrate the FBI and send information back to Russia. And, as you probably have figured out, I also moonlight with the Russian mob in South Florida. It's been a lucrative friendship. I watch their back and feed them information and they keep me, well, let's just say that I'm well taken care of", Banks explained.

As Banks finished speaking, he motioned to one of the guards. He picked up a chair and placed it beside Sophia, then shoved me into it.

"Tie him to the chair", Banks commanded, "But first, take his gun and search him for other weapons."

The guard reached under my shirt and took the gun. Then he started to pat me down. A few seconds later he found the knife I had strapped to my leg. When he finished, he tied my hands and feet with duct tape before wrapping rope around me and the chair several times. It was so tight I could barely breathe.

"So, what's the plan here Banks?", I said pissed off.

"It's simple Cole. You and Sophia are about to die."

"Why Banks? You twisted fuck! What did we ever do to you?", I screamed.

"What did you ever do to me?", Banks asked in a calm tone.

"You and I have worked together for years, Cole, and I never wanted to have to deal with you but your skills were useful to the FBI. Do you have any idea how hard I had to work to keep you away from my business dealings? Do you have any idea how condescending you were towards me all these years? All those fucking bags of Snickers that you insisted on having sent as part of your payment. We both know you did that just to be an annoying little bastard. Do you have any idea how badly that pissed me off? Do you know how many times I wanted to have my friends in the mob put a bullet in your head and throw you into the ocean?", Banks asked rhetorically.

Banks seemed like he was in a talkative mood, so I decided to keep pressing him.

"What about Simon, Banks, why did you kill him?", I asked angrily.

"Simon got himself killed. He never knew that I was Russian or that I was the one orchestrating all of this. But he was an intelligent man that was working on technology that would have been very useful to the Russian government. Could you imagine the edge it would have given us if his research could have increased the intelligence of our leaders beyond what is naturally human? Or if our leaders could live abnormally long by today's standards?", Banks explained regretfully.

"Simon had a few vices, as I'm sure you found out. A weakness for gambling was the worst one. The worse one for him that is. For us, that made him the perfect target. The Russian government worked with the mob to arrange for Simon to be given access to underground mob casinos and generous credit lines. He never suspected it was a setup until it was too late. When he got deep into debt, we owned him", Banks explained.

"So, we were right, he was being forced to work for you. That explains the Russian equipment in his lab.

So, what happened Banks, did Simon finally realize why Russia wanted his research and refuse to work anymore?", I asked.

"He refused to cooperate after he connected the dots. We suspected that he had finished his research but was stalling and had hidden it from us", Banks continued.

"So, you did the only logical thing and had your goons break into his office looking for the completed research", I interrupted.

"That's right, we wanted what was ours. When we couldn't find it, the decision was made that Simon was to be eliminated and to cut our losses. As an added bonus I came up with the idea to frame you for his murder. Two birds with one stone, you might say", Banks added with an evil laugh.

"Simon told me about the break in and asked for help since he knew I was in law enforcement. I took that opportunity and suggested that you might be helpful with figuring out what, if anything, was taken since Miami PD wasn't helpful", Banks continued.

"We, of course, had his phones bugged so when he wanted to meet with you after hours, it was the perfect opportunity to put the plan into action and get rid of you both. Unfortunately, my men got inter-rupted by Miami PD before they could finish the job.

Otherwise, you'd be rotting inside a prison cell right now for killing Simon", Banks said coldly.

"And after you failed to frame me, you tried to do the same to Kaden?", I asked pointedly.

"We needed to give the police a murderer so they would close the case and stop looking into it. I didn't expect you to care enough to clear Kaden of the crime. When you did, and then discovered Simon was in debt to the mob, you signed your own death sentence too", Banks explained.

"And that's when you decided to try to blow us up?", I asked.

"I swear to God, Cole, I think you have nine lives. I still don't know how you survived that. That's why we kidnapped your hot little girlfriend, to lure you here and to finish you both off, once and for all", Banks said smiling.

"This time I will take care of you two myself. And, Cole, this time your nine lives will be up."

Banks signaled to his men and one of them pressed a button on the wall. A motor started to run, and we saw two chains start to come down from the ceiling.

"Cole, you'll notice that those two chains are hanging over a stainless-steel container in the corner. What you can't see is that the container is filled to the top with acid. Do you know what acid does to the human body?", Banks asked.

I nodded.

"Shortly, there won't be anything left of you two. No evidence you were ever here, and I will never have to deal with you again. This will be my payment Cole, my bag of Snickers", Banks said evilly.

Banks again signaled to his two men. They picked up Sophia and I and carried us up the stairs and on to the metal walkway high above the container.

When we reached the top, Bank's men took the chains and wrapped it around our chairs.

"I have good news for you Cole, you'll get to live a little longer than your girlfriend. I want you to watch her die first", Banks said.

"You son of a bitch! When I get out of this chair-", I started to say before a punch in the kidney from Bank's goon stopped me mid-sentence.

"You won't be getting out of here Cole. You and Sophia have reached the end of the line", Banks said.

Bank's men lifted us over the railing, and we dangled about twenty feet above the large container of acid.

"Oh, and Cole, just to drag this out and make you suffer a little more, when my men press that button on the wall, you'll both be lowered little by little until, well..."

Banks paused for dramatic effect.

"You get the picture Cole", Banks said pleased with himself.

"So, it's to be torture then?", I said.

"That's right", Banks answered.

He motioned to one of his men and he pressed a button on the wall. The sound of a motor started, and Sophia started to lower down towards the acid.

"Enjoy watching your girlfriend die Cole, I know I will", Banks said laughing.

Thirty seconds later my button was pressed, and I slowly began my descent into the vat of acid.

I looked down to Sophia and said, "I'm sorry guapa."

A single tear rolled down Sophia's face.

24

I felt the jerk of the chain every few seconds as it lowered us closer and closer to our horrible deaths. Banks and his men were standing in the middle of the warehouse watching our descent with eager anticipation.

Suddenly, out of the corner of my eye, I saw movement. I turned my head for a clearer view.

It was Marko! He was sticking his head out from a hallway that led into the main warehouse floor. He saw both Sophia and I dangling from our chains then glanced at Banks and his men before scanning the upper floors.

Marko pulled a gun from his holster and fired.

BOOM!

The shot echoed in the room and I heard the unmistakable thud of a bullet hitting flesh.

One of Banks guards fell to the floor, dead.

Banks and the other guard pulled their weapons and spun around, firing shots wildly.

Marko got off another shot, but it missed, and I heard the bullet hit the concrete wall not five feet from us.

The guard ran for cover behind the acid container and I watched Banks run toward the warehouse office.

"Take care of him!", Banks screamed.

The guard nodded and fired off shots in Marko's direction.

Sophia and I dangled above the gun fight, helpless, while lowering closer and closer to the container of acid. Sophia was less than three feet above it now!

Silence filled the room as both Marko and the guard were waiting for the other to make a move. The guard, finally tired of waiting, leaned out from behind the container and took aim.

Marko was ready and as soon as he saw the guard move into the clear, he squeezed the trigger.

BOOM!

The guard jerked backwards as the bullet hit him in the chest and fell to the floor, dead.

"Marko, get up here! There is a button on the wall to stop us from lowering!", I screamed.

Marko raced across the floor and up the metal stairs. His footfalls echoed across the room.

"Sophia first! Hit the button on the right!", I screamed to Marko.

Marko found the button and I heard the motor screech to a halt and start to reverse.

Sophia was quickly being pulled up towards Marko. As she reached the top, he grabbed her and pulled her over the railing, disconnecting the chain and untying her hands.

"OK amigo, time to save your sorry ass again!", Marko yelled to me.

Marko turned and was about to press the button when a shot rang out!

I strained to look up. When I did, I saw Marko clutching his shoulder! Then I looked down and saw Banks standing in the middle of the floor pointing a gun at me!

"Goodbye Cole", Banks said as he pulled the trigger.

Click.

Click. Click. Click.

"Goddamn it!", Banks screamed.

There were no bullets left in his gun!

Banks threw his gun to the ground and ran down the hallway and out of sight.

"Marko, are you ok? Press that button! Now! I have to go after Banks!", I screamed.

Marko got to his feet, in obvious pain, and pressed the button. Within ten seconds I was at the top and Sophia pulled me over to safety.

She untied me and I placed my hand on Sophia's face.

"Take care of Marko, guapa, I'm going after that son of a bitch Banks!", I said and then ran down the stairs as fast as I could.

"Cole!", Marko yelled.

I looked up and he tossed me his gun.

"You'll need that", he said as I nodded my thanks.

I raced down the hallway and out of the warehouse, then stopped to looked around to see where Banks had gone. I spotted him as he was getting into a black Range Rover and about to make a run for it!

I needed a car!

I looked around and saw two sport cars and a Ford F-150. I ran to the sports cars first, both locked. Then over to the Ford. The window was down, and I reached in and opened the door. Hoping for the best I checked the console for a key but found nothing! Then I pulled down the sun visor and a key dropped into my lap. What luck!

I started the Ford and slammed my foot down on the accelerator. The truck sprang into action towards Banks!

Banks had turned onto NW 145th Street and was heading deeper into the airport. I watched as his Range Rover jumped an embankment and was about to enter runway 12!

I followed Banks onto the runway and pressed the accelerator all the way to the floor. I felt the truck lurch forward and it collided with the back bumper of the Range Rover. The high center of gravity on the Range Rover didn't like the nudge and the back of the Range Rover started to fishtail.

I hit the accelerator again and rammed the back of Bank's SUV a second time. This time causing it to fishtail violently before the left side tires came off the ground. The SUV flipped and rolled six or seven times before coming to a stop in the middle of the runway!

I slammed on the breaks and jumped out of the truck. With gun in hand I ran towards the wreckage.

The door of the upside-down SUV opened slowly. A bloodied Banks fell out and was now laying face-up on runway 12.

"Banks!", I screamed with my gun pointed at him, "Don't move! Stay on the ground!"

I slowly approached Banks. He looked up at me, blood running from the corner of his mouth.

"Why won't you just die, Cole?", he said coughing.

I closed my eyes and took a deep breath, "Not today Banks."

When I opened my eyes, I saw Banks was drawing a gun he had hidden and was about to pull the trigger. I fired off three quick shots into his chest.

I watched the gun fall from his hand and then his arm fell to the ground.

It was finally over.

Sirens rang out and the sight of police cars roaring down the runway towards me came into view.

Seconds later a dozen police cars surrounded me, and uniformed officers were screaming at me to drop my gun and lay down on the ground.

I did as they commanded.

A Miami PD officer kicked my gun away, handcuffed me and read me my rights. They got me to my feet and placed me in the back of a squad car.

Five minutes later an unmarked car arrived, and Detective Smith got out. He walked to the squad car holding me and tapped on the window to get my attention.

"I heard it was you, what the hell happened here?", he asked as he opened the squad car door.

"It's a long story", I answered.

"Well, you'll have as much time as you need to tell it to me in detail at police headquarters. I believe you are familiar with how it works already", Detective Smith said as he helped me out of the squad car.

"That I am. Sophia and Marko are at a warehouse on the west side of the airport. Marko was shot in the shoulder and Sophia and I were nearly killed. Can you make sure they are alright?", I asked.

"We'll take care of them", Detective Smith reassured me as we walked to his car.

"Get in", Smith said.

Then we headed off to the police station.

25

Several hours later, Detective Smith walked back into the interrogation room.

"Well, Cole, unbelievably your whole story checks out. I would have never believed that the murder of a scientist would lead to you taking down a Russian spy in the FBI who was working with the Russian mob in South Florida. You do realize you are a hero, right?", Detective Smith asked.

"I don't know about the hero part, but I am glad this is all over with", I said modestly.

Detective Smith took a key out of his pocket and released me from my handcuffs.

"I assume this means I'm free to go?", I asked.

"It does."

"What about Marko and Sophia?", I asked.

"We found both of them right where you said they would be. Marko was taken to the hospital and is fine. The bullet passed right through his shoulder. They patched him up and he will be released soon. Sophia is here waiting for you."

Detective Smith led me out of interrogation and into the lobby. A happy Sophia ran up to me and gave me a huge hug.

"I'm so glad you are OK papi", she said, "Are you free to go?"

"He is but there is a horde of reporters outside that want to talk to him", Detective Smith said, "You should probably tell them something."

I spent the next hour talking to reporters who asked the same questions over and over, while being called a hero and having picture after picture taken.

As we wrapped up, I took the phone out of my pocket and dialed Marko, not sure if he would be able to answer.

"I hope you don't need any more help, Connor, I don't think I can take it", Marko said laughing as he answered the phone.

I laughed too.

"No, I don't. I was just calling to check on you. How are you feeling?", I asked.

"Like some asshole shot me, that's how I'm feeling. But they tell me I'm going to be fine", he said.

"I'm glad to hear that. Listen, Marko, I wanted to thank you. If it weren't for you, Sophia and I would probably be dead. Thank you.", I said sincerely.

"That's what friends are for. That and repaying me with top shelf liquor for the rest of my life", he said.

"Anything you want, I think you more than earned it. There is one thing that I can't figure out though. How did you know where we were?", I asked.

"Well, I, uh, I might have hacked the login to your iPhone. I've been keeping an eye on you two. When I called the hospital and they told me that you had ran out of there, I figured the worst had happened. And I was right", Marko explained, "So, I checked out your iPhone's GPS location and couldn't figure out why you were at a warehouse near the airport. I figured I should get over there as fast as I could."

"I'm not even going to ask how you hacked my phone. But for now, I'll just say that I'm glad you did. Get some rest and we'll see you soon", I said as I ended the call.

Sophia took my hand as we walked into the fresh, early morning Miami air and sat down on a bench away from the chaos of reporters.

"You realize that you are famous now, right? A local, down on his luck, private investigator that took down a Russian spy posing as an FBI agent", Sophia said, trying to let it sink in.

"Everyone will know your name by this time tomorrow", she added.

"Yeah, you're probably right and I'm not sure how comfortable I feel about that. Ever since I lost the company I owned, I've enjoyed my anonymity down here in paradise", I said.

Sophia looked up at me sympathetically.

"I've been thinking, why don't we leave and get away from all of this for a while", I suggested.

"Like a vacation?", Sophia said excitedly.

"Yeah, a long vacation. We'll sell the land the condo was on and just disappear for a while. Any suggestions where?", I asked.

"You bet I do. How about Paris? Oh, wait, maybe Rome. Or London, or maybe some nice island in the Caribbean?", Sophia suggested unable to decide on one.

"Tell you what, let's go to our new Miami Beach office, clean up and get some sleep. Then we can go straight to the airport. We'll look at the departures list and the first one we see that looks interesting is the one we'll take. How's that sound?"

"That sounds perfect. Vamos!", Sophia said.

I smiled at Sophia, "Yes, let's go."

ALSO BY BRYAN PEABODY

If you enjoyed this story, check out my latest release:

Deep Blue Betrayal

EPILOGUE

I hope you have enjoyed reading this book, as well as getting to know Connor, Sophia, Marko and the rest of the characters in this story. It brought me great joy creating each personality as well as researching the story and places described in these pages.

It's worth pointing out that all the places that served as locations for this book are real. Although some have been embellished or changed slightly to make a more interesting story.

Over the past couple of years, my wife and I have visited each of the locations in the book on our trips to Miami, which has helped me to describe it to you much more accurately. I owe her a debt of gratitude for putting up with me while I looked around each place, thought about how it fit in the story and for allowing me to bounce ideas off her. She has been a tremendous help during the writing process.

The storyline about implanting RFID devices under employees' skin is also real and was recently in the news (depending on when you are reading this). I'd encourage you to Google it and read about it for yourself. Also worth a Google is trans-humanism, if you are interested in such things. It's a topic that will probably fascinate (and maybe terrify) you, as it did me.

Recently, I was asked how much of this story was drawn from my own life. At the time, I hadn't considered exactly how much I drew from my own life while writing this story. The short answer is simple, a lot.

The somewhat longer answer is that I drew from all areas of my personal experiences in writing this book. My twenty-one years of experience as a software engineer were used for the technical parts of this book. Although I did tone the tech talk down so it would be accessible to a broader audience.

The Spanish words and phrases used throughout this book have come from my ten years of self-study of the Spanish language. Language learning, in general, has become one of my favorite hobbies and I enjoyed being able to put it to use on the pages of this book.

My desire to travel and see the world was also very present in this book. Many of the places that Connor and Sophia visited in this story have been places that my wife and I have visited as tourists, or in the case of South Miami Hospital, a place where I spent three days of our first trip to Miami after getting a kidney stone. The doctors and nurses there took such good care of me, I wanted to show my gratitude by including them in this book, however brief.

I also must admit that I have a deep-down desire, like Connor, to throw caution to the wind, escape everything and disappear into the privacy of some sunny and sandy location until the end of my days. In a way, you might say that I'm living that dream through Connor on the pages of this book.

Finally, but certainly not least, thank you for buying, reading, and supporting my work.

THANK YOU

Thank you for purchasing and reading Murder in Magic City. I truly hope it has entertained you and that you have enjoyed the story.

As an independent author I do all the writing, editing, proof reading and publicity myself. As you can imagine it's a lot of hats to wear and it's difficult to stand out in a very crowded marketplace. But you, my valued reader, can help tremendously by leaving a review on Amazon, Goodreads or any other place where you purchase books.

If you would like to keep up with news about future Connor Cole books, author book signings or author news, please join the mailing list. I send out free chapters of new books, news about the author and special sales on all my books.

Mailing list: https://www.bryanpeabody.com/newsletter/